THE AMISH COWBOY'S MISTAKE
AMISH COWBOYS OF MONTANA
BOOK VIII

ADINA SENFT

The Amish Cowboy's Mistake / Adina Senft—1st ed.

ISBN 978-1-963929-00-3 R082724

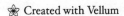 Created with Vellum

IN THIS SERIES
AMISH COWBOYS OF MONTANA

CAST OF CHARACTERS
THE AMISH COWBOY'S MISTAKE

The Amish Cowboy's Mistake follows the second branch of the Miller family, recently moved from their New Mexico ranch to Mountain Home, Montana. Rachel Miller is the widow of Marlon Miller, Reuben's brother. She is first cousin to the Zook brothers, Willard and Hezekiah (and yes, she too despairs of those two ever getting married).

The Millers at the Wild Rose Amish Inn

- Rachel Zook Miller and Luke Hertzler (engaged)
- Tobias Miller, widower, father of twins Gracie and Benny
- Gideon Miller
- Seth Miller
- Susanna Miller

The Millers on the Circle M Ranch

- Reuben and Naomi Glick Miller
- Daniel and Lovina Wengerd Lapp Miller, Joel
- Adam Miller and Kate Weaver (engaged)
- Zach Miller and Ruby Wengerd (engaged)
- Malena Miller and Alden Stolzfus (courting)
- Noah and Rebecca Miller King
- Joshua and Sara Fischer Miller, Nathan
- Deborah Miller (age 1)

THE AMISH COWBOY'S MISTAKE

❧ I ❧

MOUNTAIN HOME, MONTANA

Thursday, May 26

"WELCOME to the Wild Rose Amish Inn. I'm Susanna Miller." She had come out on the porch to greet the guests arriving this afternoon—a pair of *Englisch* ladies dressed in jeans and shirts tied at the waist by their sleeves, as the day was warm.

"Why, thanks. Glad to be here." The taller woman smiled, taking her in—sage green dress, black kitchen apron, white bucket-shaped *Kapp*, her curly hair twisted away from her face and tucked under the brim. "Fish and Game says the creek there at the bottom of the lawn is open. What's biting?"

Susanna was a cattleman's daughter who knew how to birth, brand, and drive a cow. But in the week since the Inn had opened for business, she'd had to learn more about fish than she'd ever needed to before. Or wanted to.

"Mostly brookies," she replied, "and they're using pale morning duns at sunup, and elk hair caddises in late afternoon and evening."

The shorter woman's disappointment showed in her eyes. "We didn't bring caddises."

"Not to worry," Susanna said cheerfully, leading them inside. "My brothers tie them. For a dollar fifty each you can catch the limit, and my mother will fry them up for your breakfast."

Both ladies laughed. "Now, this is what I call a full service inn."

"Not Sunday, though," Susanna said over her shoulder as she led them up the stairs to the guest rooms. "That will be a cold breakfast, since we'll be leaving for our church service at eight and we won't be back until midafternoon." Mamm wouldn't, at least. Susanna and her brothers would be at the Bar K, the ranch run by Josiah and Kathryn Keim, all day, with singing in the evening.

Heaven help her.

She shook herself back to business. "Here you are, in number one, first room on the right. Make yourselves comfortable. There is a Thermos flask of coffee in the dining room and a plate of cookies, so just help yourselves. Feel free to wander around the property, or have a look at the town. I hope you don't mind chickens."

"Not a bit," the tall woman said. "That was one of the things that made us book here for Memorial weekend, and not that big place down the county highway a bit. What's it called? Diamond something."

"The Rocking Diamond is a dude ranch," Susanna said. "They're really good at thousand-thread-count sheets and trail rides up into the mountains for corporate retreats. We only opened last week, but we like to think we're a home away from home for anglers or a family or a honeymooning couple."

"How many threads in your sheets?" the shorter one asked,

smoothing a hand over the quilt on the bed. "Not that I care when I can sleep under something as beautiful as this. Did you make it?"

"I wish. No, my cousin Malena did, at the Circle M Ranch." The quilt was one of Susanna's favorites. "She calls it *Summer Surprise*." The yellows and greens could have been a geometric wheel of triangles and chains ... or a bouquet of brown-eyed Susans if you squinted and looked at it sideways. Malena's quilts were like that. Always more than one thing going on.

"I'm glad you put us in this room," the lady said, dimples denting her cheeks. "Come on, Sandra. Coffee and cookies, and then we'll stroll the town until the sun's over the yardarm."

Susanna didn't know what a yardarm was, but as long as her customers were happy, then she was, too.

"Wait—Merrill—" Sandra leaped to the window, which overlooked the lawn, mostly, and part of their parking lot.

At the other end of their bridge was Creekside Lane, the narrow road that took them past the home of their cousins Willard and Hezekiah Zook, where Luke Hertzler was boarding until he and Mamm decided on a wedding date.

"What on earth? There are cattle all over the place!"

"It's spring turnout," Susanna said, happy to be on firm ground once more. "Let's go outside—you can watch them pass from the patio."

The Keims and Eichers were turning out today. The two ladies followed her outside and around the corner of the wrap-around veranda to the brick patio that Luke had restored for Mamm. Sunny and her six chicks took fright at the commotion and bolted under the upturned wheelbarrow. And here came the cattle down Creekside Lane, lowing and rocking and calves darting every which way.

"Cowboys!" Sandra whipped a phone out of her pocket and took some pictures. "Who knew there were Amish cowboys?"

"There are Amish dairy farmers," Merrill pointed out. "Cows are cows, right? Susanna, where are they all going?"

"The men are taking them up to their allotments. The cattle spend the summer up on the mountains, eating grass and getting fat, before we round them up and bring them back down on Labor Day weekend. That's when they go to market, and when the ranchers make most of their money."

Merrill snapped a couple of pictures as well. She asked Susanna a question, but she hardly heard it in the racket of thundering hooves, mooing ... and the sudden pounding of her heart.

There he was, and here she stood as though she'd been waiting for him. And now it was too late to turn and run into the house.

Stephen Kurtz rode easily in the saddle, his chambray blue shirt a contrast to his black work pants and suspenders. He still rode Clancy, Dat's black cutting horse—the horse Mamm had sold him because none of them had the heart to ride him after Dat died. Stephen had already got himself the peaked Siksika Valley straw hat the men wore here, halfway between a traditional Amish hat and a fedora.

Don't let him look. Don't let him see you gawking at him like you want him back.

The *gut Gott* had mercy on her. Stephen didn't look, mostly because his whole concentration was focused on keeping the cattle in the right-hand lane of the highway as the herd made the turn. Her attention was yanked off him when one of the cowboys whistled, a piercing signal that meant, *Hilfe mich!*

Without thinking, she leaped over their newly planted raised beds and ran into the parking lot, where a calf was skidding from one side to the other, clearly panicked at losing his mother. Any second now he'd kick and put a dent in the shiny bumper of one of their guests' vehicles.

Susanna whistled in short bursts through her teeth and whipped off her kitchen apron, waving it as she closed in on the calf at a dead run. It took off like a shot back through the gap where their gate hung open between clumps of wild rose bushes, leaping right over the cattle guard it had somehow managed to avoid the first time. A prayer of thanks puffed out of her as she gripped the gate and swung it closed. Half the herd had made it around the turn now.

The cowboy on point—one of the Eicher brothers—lifted a gloved hand with a grin. *"Denki!"* he hollered before he joined the flow once more, yipping and guiding the cattle in the way they should go.

She joined her guests on the patio, disheveled and panting, to find Sandra squatted down having a conversation with Sunny, the mother hen who had adopted the Inn soon after they'd moved in. Merrill was taking pictures of her with the chicks. Since neither humans nor cattle seemed inclined to attack, Sunny led the chicks into an unplanted raised bed to dust bathe. Smiling, Susanna left the ladies to pull up garden chairs and watch.

In the hallway, where it was cool, she took a moment get her breath. Then she collected two mugs, the Thermos, and the cookies, and took them outside to the little round patio table.

"How do you say thank you in Amish?" Sandra asked, smiling up at her.

"Pennsylvania Dutch," Merrill corrected her.

"We say *denki*," Susanna told them.

"Well then, *denki* for the cookies." Sandra bit into one.

5

"Chocolate chip. My favorite. This has been quite the exciting afternoon. I wonder what else the Wild Rose Amish Inn has in store for us this week?"

Merrill laughed. "Don't count your chickens before they're hatched."

Susanna couldn't help watching the last of the cattle disappear down the road out of sight. Truer words had never been spoken.

She'd counted her chickens once. Had her dreams.

And every one of them had been wrecked, fragile as any egg dropped by a careless hand.

THE INN WAS FULL BY EVENING, THE TWO ANGLERS BEING the last of the long-weekend guests to arrive. The anglers bunking in room four had been with them since opening day last weekend, and one of them had told Susanna point blank he'd be happy to stay there all summer if it weren't for the job and the family waiting for him.

Which was an odd sort of compliment, but she understood what he meant.

She hadn't wanted to leave New Mexico and start a new life. She'd wanted the life she'd nearly had—ranching on the place she and her brothers had a share in, and being Stephen's wife. But when he'd pulled up stakes and left without so much as a good-bye, and the last Amish family but themselves and the bishop's had left the Ventana Valley to move back home where there was land and prospects and a bigger church, the writing had been on the wall. Their bishop and his wife had promised to stay until Rachel could make arrangements to sell the ranch, and then they'd packed up and left, too.

When she'd sold up, the Miller family had moved here lock, stock, and barrel before spring breakup. None of them had any idea how to run a bed-and-breakfast inn, but as Mamm said when she'd told them she was going to buy the ramshackle place, "It can't be all that different from cooking and cleaning for a family, can it?"

Ach, ja, it could, but Susanna found herself liking it. Even before the renovations were complete and she had her own room, she liked the Siksika Valley, loved the fact that her cousins were only five miles away instead of three days on the train, even loved being adopted by a runaway chicken.

And then Stephen had arrived in the valley and spoiled everything upside down and backwards.

Why? she groaned to herself for the fiftieth time as she tied her apron and went into the kitchen. Why here instead of any one of the dozens of Amish communities all over the country?

She browned hamburger, mixed up an Upside-Down Pizza Casserole for supper, and put it in the propane oven to bake. Well, she knew why. Stephen was a ranch foreman, and a fine one at that. The number of states where a ranch foreman could get work was pretty much limited to the west, and if he wanted to live in an Amish community, the list shortened to Colorado and Montana. It was just bad luck that he'd chosen the second.

Had he known she was here?

That question kept her awake at night. He'd be in church on Sunday, since they were now in the same district. It would be the first time she'd seen him since he'd left the Four Winds Ranch last autumn, leaving Mamm in the lurch. She and Mamm had to pitch in to vaccinate and tag the new calves with Tobias, Gideon, and Seth—her least favorite job in the world.

Where had he been all this time?

Had he thought of her even once?

"Stop it!" she told herself, and got busy washing the dishes. Questions like that were pointless. They weren't getting back together—even a little *Kind* only had to put its hand too close to the stove once to know not to do it a second time.

No, she would be polite and cool and show no sign that she wanted to be more than his sister in Christ ever again.

The only people who knew about their former relationship were her family and her cousin Emily Kuepfer out on Prince Edward Island. She and Emily had become good friends since the Kuepfers had come for Christmas last year, and kept up a regular correspondence. If sometimes their letters sounded more like a mutual aid society than anything else, well, that was what friends were for. Susanna had the Stephen fiasco, and Emily's courtship with a boy out there had ended badly, too. Each understood the other, and Susanna had a standing invitation for a long visit. All she had to do was use the cell phone in Mamm's desk drawer to call and let them know she was coming, and they would meet the train.

There was something comforting about knowing she could flee to the other side of the continent if things got too uncomfortable. What Mamm would think about this plan she didn't know. But at least she had a plan.

The Inn only served breakfast and box lunches to its guests, not dinner. They'd decided that early on, because feeding Tobias and his twins Gracie and Benny, her other two brothers, Mamm, and herself was enough of a job. Luke usually came for dinner with them, too. It didn't take long for the table to fill up in the family parlour behind its privacy door.

At five o'clock, she put the Bisquick crust on the casserole and when it came out, golden and smelling delicious, Benny groaned. "I'm so *hungreeeee*," he moaned as though he'd gone to school without breakfast *and* lunch. Pizza casserole was his favorite.

"Grace first," Tobias reminded him.

They all bowed their heads in a silent grace, and when he raised his head, Tobias dished up Benny's plate. Susanna caught Luke smiling to himself, as though his heart was healing enough to allow him a few good memories of dinnertimes past.

"So all our guests have arrived, then?" Mamm asked Susanna as she passed the salad to Luke. She'd been out at the Circle M for Sisters' Day with Naomi, Rebecca, Lovina, and Malena. Susanna would have gone, too, except that someone had to be here to welcome Merrill and Sandra.

"Yes, we have a full house right through the weekend." Susanna helped herself to the casserole, then passed it to Seth. "The ladies in room one even got to see the Eicher and Keim herds turn out. A calf got into the parking lot and it was sheer luck I was outside and able to shoo it back where it belonged."

Seth whistled. "A panicked calf and shiny *Englisch* cars don't mix."

"The ladies are hoping to buy some elk hair caddises," she told her brothers. "With the houseful we have, you'd better stock up."

Both Gid and Seth brightened at the prospect. "Some mayflies, too," Gideon mused, the wheels in his head clearly already spinning. "I bet they'll go through a lot of those by next week, if they're fishing farther afield."

"Luke and I were talking," Mamm said after a glance at her intended, in a tone that was way too casual, "and we wondered what you *Kinner* would think if we got married in October."

"What we *Kinner* think matters less than what you both think," Tobias said with a smile.

"Not to mention, what does the bishop think?" Gideon asked.

"As it happens, I spoke with him this afternoon," Luke said.

Susanna rolled her eyes. "So *that's* why you went to the Circle M. I think not one thing got accomplished on Sisters' Day except wedding plans."

"That's not true," Mamm said. "We did some quilting."

"Two inches," Susanna confided in a whisper to Gracie. "Maybe three."

"A whole feathered border for Malena's newest quilt," Mamm retorted with dignity. "But after Luke came over and told us the bishop could marry us at Willard and Zeke's place on October fourth, we sort of forgot about quilting."

Luke took their laughter in stride. "With the barn raising next month, we'd have it fitted up and able to host the church by October. But Will and Zeke want to do this for us, being Rachel's cousins and my landlords, as it were."

"I'd be happy if you got married tomorrow," Susanna said. "But October would be *wunderbaar*—and if you do it early enough, it might not even snow."

Mamm reached over to squeeze Susanna's hand. "Luke and me, we've weathered our share of storms. I reckon even if I had to snowshoe over to the Zook place, nothing would keep me from marrying him."

Susanna's eyes filled with tears—the happy kind. Oh, in recent weeks she'd had plenty of mixed-up feelings where Mamm and Luke were concerned. But Luke himself had won Susanna over with the kind of steadfast love for Mamm that Dat had when he was alive ... and that she wanted for herself one day.

As unlikely as that prospect was at the moment.

2

THE BAR K RANCH

Sunday, May 29

STEPHEN KURTZ HAD SLEPT in many a bunkhouse, from worst (a shared room in a falling-apart trailer in Wyoming) to best (the comfortable foreman's cabin on the Four Winds Ranch in New Mexico). He fastened the hidden snaps in the placket of his white Sunday shirt and considered the Bar K bunkhouse, where the other Amish hands were also dressing for church. He didn't have his own apartment, but as foreman, he had the big bed in front of the window at the far end, and a double wide closet for his gear.

None of the men here wore cowboy boots to church, so he followed their example and put on his black shoes. A black weskit and a black felt Siksika hat completed the ensemble that looked pretty much the same for an Amish man no matter where he was on the continent. Stephen descended the inside staircase that took him into a short corridor with a door on each end—one into the barn, and one out to the yard. Church would be in the Keim home, and the near pasture was already half full of buggies. Back in Holmes County, he remembered being one of the young ostlers, so delighted to be chosen to unhitch the horses and lead them into the adjoining meadow. Then after leaving school at fourteen, he'd hung around with the *Youngie*, like that crowd of young men there, elbowing and joshing each other as they snuck peeks at the young women exchanging news on the wraparound porch.

But now he held a place of responsibility on the Bar K ranch. He might see these young men at singing tonight, but his place before church was elsewhere. He ambled over to where his employer, Josiah Keim, and some of the other ranchers and foremen stood in a circle near the barn doors, greeting each other and catching up on what was new in the two weeks since the last church Sunday.

Stephen himself fell into that category—the new guy. He was introduced to several of them, but one face was so familiar it needed no introduction.

"Tobias Miller." He gripped Susanna's brother's hand in a firm shake. "*Gut* to see you. Why did I think you'd be going to church with your cousins on the Circle M?"

"We did while we were living there, but when we moved into the Inn, the bishop put us in this district. Good to see you, Stephen."

Tobias was not the kind of man who would run his mouth in public. But curiosity lay in his eyes. Stephen wasn't certain if it was curiosity about how he'd found his way here, or the kind that involved Tobias's sister.

To Stephen's relief, Josiah spoke up. "The bishop's wife over to the Ventana Valley is a cousin of mine," he told the group. "When she heard my foreman had moved on, it didn't take but a minute to call and tell me that if I didn't snap him up, I'd be sorry. And she was right. Turnout went so smoothly you'd think we were actually trying."

Stephen smiled modestly at the praise. "You've got a pretty experienced crew here. I was just glad to be one of the hands. We'll ride up the mountain tomorrow to make sure all the calves have mothered up and no one has got lost."

"But that's tomorrow." Tobias had been keeping an eye on his twins, who were reaching through the fence to pet the horses' noses. "Today belongs to the Lord, and I'd better round up my *Kinner* before the teenaged boys there beat us inside."

Stephen smiled, remembering the days when, with the boys, he went in last. Now he walked in with the men and found his place with the singles. Since they sat in order of age, he was toward the back, though Tobias, as a widower, sat with the married men, Benny at his side. He watched Gracie find her grandmother on the women's side.

Honest, he tried not to look any farther. Because of course Susanna would be with the married women. Probably with a *Boppli* in her lap and one playing quietly on the floor.

He tried. And failed. And it didn't matter anyway, because she wasn't with the married women. Or the young mothers sitting in the back row. He'd seen that when he'd walked in.

Surely she wouldn't be among the single women. Not Susanna. Not after all these months. She would have found someone else—got married—not—

Like a homing pigeon going to its roost, or a magnet finding iron, his disbelieving gaze landed on her, sitting on the bench between the visiting Keim cousins, Sharon and Bethany.

He hadn't seen her in a year, and yet his heart gave the same thump of recognition it used to every morning at breakfast. Her *Kapp* was a little different now from the one the women had worn in New Mexico, and she wore a cape and apron the same color as her dress, the way the women here did, not white like Lancaster or black like the Ventana Valley. But the set of those shoulders was the same, the curl of her hair on the nape of her neck hadn't changed ... and he was pretty sure that if he got a look into those cornflower blue eyes, he'd see the same snap and fire of her zest for life.

Or the snap and fire of her intense disgust. Of betrayal. Maybe even unforgiveness.

Stephen was so rattled he was thankful when the *Lob Lied*, the second hymn, began because every Amish person knew it by heart. Which meant he could sing and pray at the same time.

Why, Lord? he implored the Almighty. *Why did You lead me here to this valley when You knew she was here? Why didn't you open up the way to Monte Vista, or Amity—or even one of the Amish communities in eastern Montana? Why guide me to this valley—this church district—this house?*

Der Herr had no answers that Stephen's jangled spirit could hear.

And if You led me here for reasons of Your own, why isn't she married and safely out of reach?

If he could have, Stephen would have put his face in his hands. He imagined himself getting up, slipping out through the kitchen door, saddling Clancy, tying on his duffel bag, and galloping away as fast and as far as the horse could take him.

But he couldn't. He could only sit here and face straight ahead and when the hymns ended and the service began, pretend to listen.

After the deacon had finished the prayer, Bishop Joe Wengerd opened his mouth and boomed, "Now faith is the substance of things hoped for, the evidence of things not seen." With a start, Stephen realized that not only

ADINA SENFT

had the *gut Gott* led him here for reasons of His own, He had a sense of humor. The Scripture today was on faith, in Hebrews 11 and 12.

Once, Susanna had been the substance of things he hoped for.

And for her, no doubt he was the evidence of things not seen—for months.

Which wasn't exactly the point Scripture was making, but it was no less true.

The bishop—a white-haired giant of a man whom Josiah inexplicably called Little Joe—read through the examples of the patriarchs and what they had done and been through their faith. Then the preacher stood to speak. Before they became patriarchs, they had been ordinary men. Like Stephen, like Tobias, like any man *Gott* had created. And faith in *Gott*'s leading had brought them safely to the conclusion of their journey, with rewards much greater than any they could ask or think.

Was that the point *der Herr* was trying to make this morning? *Be patient. Lay aside the weight of the past and run the race I have set before you, Stephen Kurtz.*

He didn't say *run away, period.* Tempting as that was. But run the course set before him, with faith that *Gott* would bring him safely through.

With Your help, I'll do my best, mei Vater, he thought unhappily. *But it isn't going to be easy.*

In fact, it would be easier to run through a snowdrift as high as his chin.

There were sixteen families in the east district, Sylvia Keim had told him. That was more than they'd had in the Ventana Valley, so would be enough for Stephen to avoid running into Susanna in the crowd if he worked at it. Little Joe raised his hand at the conclusion of the preacher's sermon and the final hymn, signifying he had an announcement. His vivid blue eyes twinkled at them all.

"This might be a little out of the usual order, but I have happy news about two of our newest members in the district. Rachel Miller and Luke Hertzler have told me of their desire to marry, and we've settled on the fourth of October this year, at Willard and Hezekiah Zook's place." He waited for the smiles and murmurs to die down. "And now, we'll enjoy our fellowship meal together."

Stephen realized that any chance of hiding had evaporated. He would be expected to approach the Miller family, shake hands with them all, and give good wishes to the newly engaged couple. The Keim family in particular would expect it —they knew he'd once worked for the Millers. Mind you, probably by now the entire valley knew that.

Der Herr was giving his faith a workout today, for sure and certain.

So while the young men set up the tables and benches inside, the greater part of the congregation surrounded Rachel and Luke outside in the May sunshine. *"Kumm mit,"* Sylvia said cheerfully, and dragged him into the crowd behind her parents.

He could be sincere in his congratulations, at least. When Rachel had lost her husband, *Gott* had opened the way for Stephen to come to the Four Winds Ranch. She'd needed someone to take charge in the worst way, and he was fresh off his first foreman's job and needed the work. Luke might be a stranger to him, but even he could see that Rachel looked like a woman restored to happiness.

"Stephen," Rachel said, her smile as warm as the summer sun. Impulsively, she took his hand between both of hers and gave it a squeeze before releasing it. "I'm so glad to see you. The Keim place suits you?"

"Down to the ground," he said. "Interesting how *Gott's wille* works—bringing us all to the valley, *ja*? And your intended, too, I hear."

"There's no one happier about that than I," Luke said, with a smile into Rachel's eyes. "I understand you were Rachel's foreman?"

"*Ja*, for almost four years," Stephen replied. In his peripheral vision, the young Keim cousins separated and behind them, Susanna started like a horse stung by a fly. Her eyes widened when she saw him talking to her mother.

"I hope we'll see something of you, Stephen," Rachel said. "Though it won't take long for you to get involved with the *Youngie* and their doings, I expect."

He opened his mouth to reply, when two small bodies barrelled into him, one on each side. "Stephen!" Benny Miller cried. "You're here!"

"I'm foreman with this outfit for as long as they put up with me." Laughing, he bent to give each twin a hug before Tobias corralled them and prepared to go in for lunch. Seth and Gideon found him then, and before he knew it, he was being borne away to sit with them instead of with the Keim family. Susanna seemed to have made friends with the Keim girls, so she went to join them at their table.

Just as well. The longer he could stave off the inevitable meeting, the better.

THE ACT OF BREATHING USED TO BE SO EASY. BUT BEING within a hundred yards of Stephen Kurtz made her all *verhud-*

delt, lungs included. Susanna hadn't expected him to be cold, or unkind, but she'd expected him to at least be civil. He could laugh with Tobias, hug the twins, congratulate her mother, and sit with her brothers—but he couldn't even say *guder mariye* to her?

Nobody liked to be ignored. But she had to admit it was almost a relief.

"Our new foreman seems nice," Bethany Keim said, practically ladling a thick layer of marshmallow peanut butter spread on a piece of homemade bread. She and her sister Sharon were cousins of the Keim siblings, come to help Kathryn and Sylvia on the ranch for the summer.

"And handsome," her sister Sharon added, sneaking a look at where Stephen sat with Gideon and Seth. "If a man is going to move into a neighborhood, it's always nice if he's good-looking."

Susanna bit into her ham, cheese, and pickle sandwich to stifle the words on the tip of her tongue. It wouldn't help to offend her new friend by teasing her about the depth of her character. Like, shallow enough to catch tadpoles in.

"He was foreman on the Miller place in New Mexico," Bethany told one of the Yoder girls across the table. "Come on, Susanna, spill the beans. What's Stephen like when he's not being a foreman? Is he seeing anyone?"

Susanna swallowed and took a drink of milk. "I don't know. He left our ranch last year and we haven't heard a word since." There, that was the right tone to take. Level. Unconcerned. "He's a *gut* foreman, for sure and certain. He'll do well for Josiah."

"I need to find out more," Sharon said, a glint of determination sparkling in her eyes. "Who would know if he's writing to anyone?"

Bethany rolled her own eyes in disgust at her sister. "Why don't you just steal his phone and read his texts? That would be easiest."

"Bethany!" Then Sharon seemed to realize she was being teased. "Oh, you. Well, I'll just make sure he chases me until I catch him, that's all. It's not every day that an eligible man hires on. Usually they're too old, or too young, or they're on *Rumspringe* and wild as coyotes, or—" She stopped as a sudden thought struck her. "He *is* baptized, isn't he, Susanna?"

"*Ja*, he is." A big bite of her sandwich prevented her from elaborating.

But the memories sparked in her head like sunlight on water. Taking baptism classes together before church every Sunday. The spring day they'd both knelt at the front of the small Ventana Valley *Gmay* and made their promises to *Gott* and His church. The hope swelling in her heart that with that step of eternal commitment, Stephen would ask her the question that would lead to an earthly commitment, too.

But within a year, he'd vanished, never to be heard from again ... until he'd turned up here a few days ago. He obviously had not been the man she thought she knew. And if he could walk away from her—he'd cared, she knew it in her soul—he wasn't likely to be the kind to open up his heart and settle down with anyone here, either.

Lieber Gott, don't let him do that. Don't make it so I have to go to his wedding to someone else.

That was up to the Almighty, but in the meantime, she had to spend the afternoon watching not only Sharon and Bethany, but all three Yoder girls *and* the two Stolzfus sisters circling Stephen like bees around a flower. A word here, a giggle there, and offer to show him where the wild strawberries grew. Susanna bit back a groan and wished she were safely in the west district, where the likelihood of seeing him would have gone down substantially. Alden Stolzfus had dropped off his mother and sisters here at the Keim place, and taken the buggy to the Circle M, since it was their off Sunday. He and her cousin Malena were courting. She should have begged a ride.

With a sigh, Susanna took refuge in the kitchen and did what Sharon and Bethany were supposed to be doing—helping Kathryn Keim do the dishes after lunch. It took a good hour, and in the meantime she had to listen to a list of all their new foreman's favorite dishes. As was customary, he ate breakfast and supper with the family, and took lunch in his saddlebag out on the range, just as he'd done in New Mexico. Not for worlds would Susanna mention that one of his favorites was her mother's Christmas salsa, so called not because it was served at Christmas, but because it was a combination of red and green chile. He'd put it on everything if he could—even beef.

Susanna reflected that now, the jars of Christmas salsa in the pantry were more likely to bring him over to the house than she was. Not that she wanted him anywhere near her.

The older folks and the families with young *Kinner* began to roll out around midafternoon, and then it became downright difficult to avoid him. Kathryn Keim chased her out of the house along with the boys taking out the benches. They'd put half in the bench wagon, and the rest would be used by the *Youngie* during supper and singing.

In desperation, she found her eldest brother. "Are you staying for singing? Want me to look after the twins?"

Tobias looked at her as if she'd gone crazy. "*Neh*, I'm not staying, and the twins are going home with me and Mamm, like usual." Then his gaze seemed to take her in more carefully.

"What's going on? Stephen hasn't said anything to you, has he?"

She sucked in a breath and glanced around to see if anyone was close enough to hear. If they were, they were too busy talking to pay attention. "No. We haven't spoken."

"It has to happen sometime."

"I know, but I'd rather it wasn't today. Maybe I'll come home with—"

"There you are!" Sylvia Keim looped an arm through hers. "My cousins were looking for you. Are—are you heading home, Tobias?" Her cheeks bloomed with color.

And Susanna realized suddenly what was going on under her nose. But she seemed to be the only one who understood what that blush meant.

Tobias said absently, "*Ja*, as soon as I can rope and tie my *Kinner*. Have you seen them?"

"They're in the pasture, trying to catch your horse." She blushed again. "At least, I hope it's your horse. With those two, you never know what they're up to."

Tobias gave her a puzzled glance, as though he'd never found this to be a problem, and with a nod, set off toward the meadow where the *Gmay*'s horses grazed.

For the space of one second, Susanna debated whether or not to tell Sylvia Keim not to get her hopes up. Tobias was still married to Lily Anne in his heart, and as far as she knew, he was a one-woman man. Besides, between herself and Mamm, Benny and Gracie were getting all the mothering they needed.

But the moment passed, and Susanna gently pulled her arm from Sylvia's. "I'll go find your cousins."

"What?" Sylvia was watching Tobias unlatch the pasture gate.

Never mind. With a sigh, Susanna walked around Fraa

Keim's massive garden, hoping the path would take her to where she'd last seen the girls. It was protected by an eight-foot deer fence, and accessible by a gate in the end closest to the house. But Susanna could see that the peas were already halfway up their teepees, and the warm weather had made Fraa Keim's six precious tomato plants bush out. Little yellow flowers were coming.

Luke had plowed and raked Mamm's garden and built the obligatory fence to keep the deer out of it. Seth had sown it with fast-growing radishes, bush beans, lettuce, kale, and chard. But their land must not get the kind of sun this ranch did on its south-facing slope—their vegetables were hardly out of the ground, and Mamm was babying her tomatoes in the raised beds on the patio, along with some raspberry canes. Susanna had put in a few blueberry bushes that might or might not be a success, but they wouldn't know until the plants were as old as the twins were now.

She turned from the garden with a huff of laughter at herself. Hope sprang eternal—especially when the blueberries wouldn't fruit for seven years. She'd be laboring for them like Jacob had for Rachel.

Thinking about blueberries and winter, she walked straight into a man coming along the path, practically bouncing off him.

"What's that smile for, Susanna Miller?" Stephen asked, reaching out with both hands to steady her.

3

HER HEAD EMPTIED OF WORDS—OF sense—of everything but the fact that his hands were warm and his green eyes were once more gazing into hers. Eyes that had haunted her dreams in good ways and bad over the past months.

And then he released her as though he'd been burned and stepped back. "Sorry," he said. "I didn't mean to startle you. I was just going to check on Clancy."

"Clancy?" Her tongue had formed a word. That was something.

"*Ja*. You know, the cutting horse I bought from Rachel?"

Breathe. "I know who Clancy is. I meant, why are you checking on him?"

"He got a little too close to a barbed wire fence yesterday. Both of us knew better. Me, mostly. I should have seen that big old piece of broken wire sticking out."

Was he babbling? Was that even possible? Could he be as nervous as she?

"Will he be okay? Did you put the—"

"*Ja*, I had ointment in the saddlebag. Same one as always. But Josiah says good old Amish B-and-W will do in a pinch."

Burn and Wound ointment was the standby in every Amish household she'd ever been in—and with the twins, they used it a lot. Cuts, burns, pulled muscles—it helped all of them.

She stood aside. "I won't keep you, then."

He smiled. Passed her. And didn't look back even once, all the way to the pasture.

Which was fine. But that didn't stop her mind from replaying every word of that conversation, every change in the tone of his voice, every nonsensical syllable she'd said, for the rest of the afternoon.

Oh, why hadn't she gone home with Tobias?

Supper was leftovers from lunch, with the addition of a big pot of chicken and dumpling soup, and generous bowls of potato chips. She did her best to talk and laugh, and maybe she got to know the other *Youngie* a little better, but she felt like a puppet—doing what was expected while in her mind, she talked nonsense to Stephen over and over. If only she could have been calm, cool, and collected! Maybe even had the sense to ask him where on earth he'd been hiding all this time.

But calm had never been possible for her, even when they were courting. Calm was for people like Sylvia Keim, who was perfectly sensible and coherent even when she talked to Tobias. Only a blush betrayed her—not that he noticed.

Susanna's entire body and mind had betrayed her. Stephen probably thought she was a complete *narre*. *Good riddance*, he would have said to himself as he went to check on his horse. *I had a lucky escape there.*

Where had that come from? Something sparked inside her —the reply of her heart to the incessant criticism of her brain.

Maybe he did think that. Maybe he didn't. The fact was, what reasonable man talked about his horse and then walked away instead of at least asking about her life—a life now so different from the one she'd had she might almost be a different person? He could simply have said he was sorry for dumping her flat. Or even apologized for the months of silence. Didn't he owe them that courtesy, at least?

Her temper, instead of getting her into trouble, for once helped her spine to straighten and her mind to climb out of its pointless spiral.

The Keim girls cleared away the plates after supper and Sylvia's youngest brother Jonathan, who had just moved back to the valley after a stint in Colorado, brought out the box of hymnbooks—the *Ausbund*, of course, but also *Mountain Laurel Echoes* and the green songbook with more modern hymns in it.

Susanna came to a decision.

It was clear that Stephen Kurtz felt nothing more for her than a Christian brother might feel for a sister. That was fine. She would not spend another second of her life pining for him. *Gott* might have brought him to the Siksika Valley for some reason known only to Himself, but He had brought her family here, too. She had a life to make that didn't include him. He'd already walked away from her once. She didn't need a second demonstration of his feelings—or lack thereof. She'd misunderstood, that was all. They'd had some fun together, and it was over, and that was that.

So. Time to look about her and take notice.

The *Youngie* in this district numbered maybe twenty. If you combined them with the ones in the west district, you might get to three dozen or so. And of those, how many were men ready to settle down?

There was the burning question. With all the attention

that Stephen had received from the girls today, Susanna had to wonder. Then again, if some of these girls had grown up with the young men, it wouldn't surprise her if they treated them like brothers instead of marriage prospects. Seth and Gideon were certainly getting their fair share of attention, as three girls made a little fuss over who was going to sit opposite them.

Susanna made her choice, and seated herself just close enough to David Yoder that he could pass her a green hymnbook. And when he did, she lifted her lashes and smiled in a thank-you.

That was all it took.

David passed her *Mountain Laurel Echoes*, too, and then said shyly, "Do you know Cora Swarey? She's from Amity—engaged to Simon Yoder from Whinburg Township?"

"She's the hymn writer, isn't she? Is Simon one of your Yoder relatives?"

"*Ja*, cousins once removed. We just got the invitation to their wedding in November. It's going to be in Colorado."

"Not Whinburg? We have cousins there, too—Melvin and Carrie Miller."

"The wedding is usually at the bride's home, *nix*? I'm just as glad. I'm not one for travel. Colorado at least is close by. Though in the winter even *close by* can be pretty far and difficult to manage."

"Just like ranching." She laughed.

"For sure and certain." He smiled, too. "Anyway, what I was getting at is that along with the invitation, Cora sent a new hymn for my sisters."

"Oh, how lovely! 'Walk a Little While' is one of my favorites of hers. Are we going to learn the new one tonight?"

"I think that's the plan." Dave craned his neck in his sister

Sallie's direction. "Looks like she has a pile of copies there." His dark brows flickered into a frown and then relaxed. "I don't know—doesn't it seem a little prideful to you? Along with your wedding invitations, to send out a hymn you wrote?"

Susanna tried not to show she was taken aback. "I don't think so. One, it's only sensible to save the stamp if you were going to send both anyway. Two, maybe she wants the guests to learn it and sing it after the wedding, before supper. And three, we all like getting her hymns. I hear that the *Youngie* sing them all over the place. Mamm showed me one that had been printed in *The Budget*, even, with a couple of suggestions for tunes people could use." She grinned. "I wonder if the *Youngie* here would pick a tune like 'Country Roads' over 'The Old Rugged Cross'?"

Now he really did frown, or maybe it was because his brother Calvin, who took up a lot of room to begin with, had knocked him with an elbow when he plunked himself down on the bench.

"Those two don't have the same kind of tune," David finally said, leaning out of range of any more stray arms and legs.

"I meant them as examples." Stephen would have known that. So would any of her brothers. "In New Mexico, we tended to pick a more modern tune instead of an old one."

"Oh."

"Hey," Calvin greeted them. "Who feels like singing?"

"I hear we have something new from Cora Swarey," Susanna told him.

"Great! Hey, Sharon—let's learn the new one."

"All in good time, Calvin. You'll get your solo soon enough." The *Youngie* laughed while Calvin turned red. Clearly, in the time she'd been here, Sharon Keim had had a little practice in managing his boisterous, clueless ways.

All the same, Sharon passed out the pages, which had been photocopied from a handwritten original. At the top was the title, *After the Fire*. At the bottom was a notation in a neat hand that must be Cora's: *Can be sung to any modern hymn with a 4/4 time signature.*

"How about that tune I tried to get you all to sing last winter?" Calvin suggested. "It's got four beats, and it's kind of western sounding."

"The one you heard at that shindig in Whinburg Township?" his sister Lydia called from her end of the table. "The one that got broken up by the sheriff when somebody set the field on fire?"

A number of eyebrows went up, including Susanna's. Maybe that was a story she didn't want to hear.

"That wasn't me," Calvin protested. "But it's a *gut* tune. Can we try it at least?"

Sharon relented. Susanna suspected both she and Lydia knew that if he heard *no* too many times, he'd start acting up. And as it turned out, the cowboy-sounding tune suited them and the valley both ... even if they had to listen to a recording on Calvin's phone in order to learn it.

> Upon the lofty mountain I proudly raised my
> hands
> All eternity this earth could show
> But the wind came up and tore at me so I could
> not stand
> I'd be flung to the rocks below.

The ground began to shake and I could not stay
    so brave
I clung to things that fell away
I flung myself to earth, there was no one come
    to save
The night had overcome the day.

Was there no one to help me, none to lend
    a hand
No word from any friendly voice?
If I could only hear a word from the Shepherd
    to the lamb
I could make a very different choice.

Now my shelter in the trees was engulfed in
    waves of flame
I could not find a way to flee
The fearsome rolling fire would surely lay its
    claim
None would know what happened to me.

There at last I heard a sound, just a whisper in
    my ear
"I am not in wind, in earth, in fire
I dwell inside your heart—let Me keep you
    safely near
Of My still, small voice you'll never tire."

Of course Calvin clapped afterward, which made Fraa
Keim look in, just long enough to make him stop. Hymns
were supposed to praise God, not man, but all the same,
Susanna was glad they'd learned it. Maybe she'd even

make a copy for Emily on PEI and enclose it in her next letter.

And then someone chose 'How Great Thou Art.' Susanna felt a thrill run down to her toes—it was Stephen's favorite *Englisch* hymn, and once, she'd secretly believed that it would be sung at their wedding. Thank goodness she'd never confided *that* to anyone.

Even though Amish singing was not supposed to reveal any one voice, except maybe that of the *Vorsinger* in the beginning, she could still hear Stephen's at the other table—a warm tenor that she could pick out of a crowd anywhere. And of course, once she'd picked it out, she couldn't *not* hear it as they went on to sing hymns and favorites from their songbooks. She'd be hearing him after she went to bed, singing in her dreams.

Around ten o'clock, people passed down their hymnbooks to be put in the boxes once more. Susanna and the others thanked the Keims and their *Youngie* for hosting, and then she went to find Seth. Since they didn't have a barn at the Wild Rose Amish Inn, and their only buggy horse was boarding at the Circle M, Mamm and Luke had taken the buggy back this afternoon. It was pretty likely that she, Seth, and Gideon could get a ride back to town with Beth and Julie Stolzfus.

Sure enough, she found Seth out in the pasture, helping Beth hitch up. Christie Petersheim stood nearby, and the two girls were talking a mile a minute to him.

Oh my. Seth was the kind who never needed to be asked to help, but he was not the boldest person in the world. He and Calvin Yoder were like the two end points on the shyness scale. Which meant it was rare indeed that Seth would talk to one girl, never mind two at once.

Clearly it was not the time for a sister to interrupt. Susanna faded into the darkness and turned down the lane of buggies, heading back to the yard, where people were congregating under the yard light and talking. Seth would be able to see her over there. Its generator muttering in the background just sounded like more conversation.

"Susanna?" Dave Yoder was backing his horse between the rails of a buggy, and she heard the jingle of harness as his horse tossed its head.

"Hi, Dave. I was just checking with my brother about a ride." Out of habit, she moved to the other side of the animal to help him buckle the harness.

"He has a buggy here?"

"No, he was going to ask the Stolzfus girls if we could ride along. It will be a little squished with five, but they live close to us. Just on the other side of the bridge."

"Maybe ..." He paused, then seemed to come to a decision. "Would it be less squished if you rode back with me? I don't have any passengers."

What were the odds Stephen was somewhere in the line of buggies, within earshot? Never mind. She had to focus on the big picture.

"*Denki*, Dave," she said. "That's very kind of you. I'll just run into the house and get my handbag and meet you in the driveway."

"Maybe take a walk down a ways," he suggested. "You know how people are."

She did know. The teasing could be daunting enough to make a young man think twice about giving a girl a ride home. But at the same time, she was making a point to a certain person. She smiled, and Dave could take that for agreement or not.

In the house, it only took a minute to collect her purse and sweater, and another minute to locate that certain person in the crowd, in the company of the Keim cousins, plus Jonathan. Susanna felt the moment when Stephen turned his head and became aware of her, like an electric charge in the air.

She strolled along the grass on the verge of the gravel drive as slowly as if she had nowhere else to be. And then Dave murmured to his horse and pulled up his buggy beside her. She climbed in amid the catcalls and whistles of the boys—including Calvin, the loudest of them all—then settled her skirts around her as Dave clicked his tongue to the horse and they lurched into motion.

That had gone rather well, if she said so herself.

"You're a slow walker." Dave turned his attention from the long lane to smile at her. "I'd hoped you'd be a little further down."

"Does it bother you, being teased like that?" she asked. "Especially when your own *Bruder* is the loudest?"

"I'm used to Calvin. He's like a blizzard. You can't do anything about him, so you just wait him out. *Neh*, I was talking about the rest of them. It gets old after a while."

She laughed. "How many girls have you driven home?"

"Well, a man has to start somewhere." He sounded a little defensive. "And you did need a ride."

"I appreciate your offering me one," she said in as soothing a tone as she could muster. "I'm sure my brothers will appreciate not having me in the Stolzfus buggy, too. So that's three grateful people."

He seemed to relax a little. "It's about four miles into town from here. We're pretty spread out. A lot of these ranches go right back into the foothills. Some even cover the bases of the mountains, right up to the tree line."

"And people still use the allotments, even with that much of their own grazing?"

"*Ja*, they do. The summer pastures are rich with grass, but when we bring the animals down, it's *gut* to have grass still available on our own places, too."

"And avoid overgrazing," she agreed. "We had the same system in New Mexico."

"It's pretty exciting here during roundup."

Another man who didn't ask her about the life she'd loved. "Our guests at the Inn thought the Keim and Eicher turnout was pretty exciting. Especially when a calf got into our parking lot and I had to chase him out. I could have used Andy, my cutting horse, that's for sure. But he's at the Circle M until after the barn raising."

"You help with the cattle?"

"Sure," she said, a little surprised. "When we're short of hands, which we have been recently, everyone has to pitch in. Don't your sisters help?"

He shook his head, slowing his horse for a stop sign. When he flapped the reins over its back, he said, "Roundup especially is the biggest event on the non-church calendar. My sisters have enough to do getting the house ready for a crowd and helping Mamm with the meal. Besides, we live in town. We keep about thirty head on Aendi Annie King's fields, but that's all."

She nodded. "On the Four Winds, it was often just us, and maybe an *Englisch* hand or two. Our church district was smaller than this one. People couldn't make a go of it unless they lucked into good land like we did. Families began to leave one by one, until in the end, it was just us and our bishop. And he wasn't a rancher—he had a store in town. So roundup was basically just our cattle, especially this last autumn."

When Stephen had waited barely two days before he'd up and left.

"That must have been hard."

"It was," she said honestly. "I loved it on the Four Winds. I'd have stayed there happily for the rest of my life. But that wasn't *Gott's wille*—especially if a person is looking to have their own home and family."

"And you are?"

"Of course," she said, surprised. Did he think her unwomanly ways extended to being permanently single?

"At least the work at the Inn is a little more suitable to an Amish woman than riding and roping."

David Yoder was beginning to rub Susanna's fur the wrong way, but she kept her tone cheerful. "We're a family of well-rounded women—we can ride and rope, as well as scrub and cook. As Mamm says, you help a calf into this world when he's born, guide him and feed him while he grows, help him out of it when he's slaughtered, and then you put him on the table to feed your family. It takes all stages to make that animal useful."

"But all those stages but the last one are men's work."

They were on the outskirts of town now, thank goodness. "Depends on your circumstances, I guess. Even the virtuous woman in Proverbs planted her own vineyard, and it says she had strong arms and hands."

"That's gardening, not cattle."

She took a deep breath and bit back what she wanted to say. "I take it you don't plan to be a rancher?"

"Me? *Neh*. Cal and I will probably take over the variety store when Dat is ready to retire."

She could just imagine Calvin Yoder in the store, going down the aisles of goods like the proverbial bull in the china shop. "Probably?"

He shrugged. "You never know what Calvin is going to do. But I already work there. Inventory is my favorite part. You know, making sure what comes in is what I ordered, getting it all out on display so it's easy for people to see and buy. That kind of thing."

"I'm sure you're good at it." A nice, orderly job for a man who had very firm ideas about everything being in its place.

"Well, here we are." He pulled up where the Inn's bridge crossed the creek, as though he expected her to jump down and open the gate on the far side. So before he could get any ideas about coming in for a cup of coffee and some cake, Susanna jumped down and turned to speak through the open door. "*Denki*, Dave. I appreciate the ride."

"I enjoyed it, too."

That was not what she'd said.

"How about if I—"

But she was already across the bridge and through the gate, which clanked as she slid the latch home behind her. "*Guder nacht*—see you soon!"

He had the goodness to watch until she was safely inside, and then she heard the buggy make the right turn on to the highway. The Yoders lived behind the variety store on a nice acreage that could be accessed through its parking lot.

Susanna leaned on the front door and took several deep breaths. She'd got what she wanted and made her point with that certain someone. But four miles in a buggy with David Yoder was a price higher than any girl should have to pay.

Monday, May 30

DEAR EMILY,

Thanks so much for yours, and for the recipe for fish chowder. If there's anything we have a lot of around here, it's fresh fish! I wonder if the guests would like a big pot of it with biscuits for breakfast. They're a fishy enough crowd—and it would make a change from things made with meat and eggs ... In any case, when the barn is finally built and we do get to host church here, it will also make a wonderful addition to the fellowship meal. Goodness knows Seth and Gideon need no excuse to get out on the river to catch the ingredients!

Well, it finally happened—the thing I've been dreading. At least I had some preparation for meeting Stephen Kurtz by seeing him at a distance. He was with the Eicher outfit and drove their herd right past the Inn, much to the excitement of the guests and the dismay of the calf that got stuck in our parking lot! I chased him out before one of his hooves was introduced to one of the guests' vehicles. Stephen never even noticed. So maybe it was a surprise to him to see me in church on Sunday. He had all morning to recover before we ate lunch, and we avoided each other quite successfully for most of the afternoon. Then I ran into him unexpectedly. No one was around. But if you were hoping for a big reunion, I'm sorry to disappoint you. We said probably six words to each other and then he walked away.

He's very good at that, as you know.

I don't mind confessing to you that this is going to be really hard on me. We're going to see each other—not only at church, but when people invite our families to dinner, when the Youngie do things together on Friday nights, at work frolics, you name it. How am I going to survive?

You know it's only going to get worse. Not only do the girls here have my brothers to moon over, but now they have Stephen—and believe me, Emily, his looks have not suffered since last year. What are the odds we hear an engagement announcement this winter?

I'm only half kidding when I ask you to keep the guest room ready for me. Mind you, the serious half knows that Mamm needs my help. Running the Inn is more work than either of us expected—the laundry *alone is like mounting a military operation once a week, since you have to send it out, and the company is forty miles away in Libby. But all the same, the blue gulf and the red sand beaches are looking mighty tempting right now.*

I must let this do. My eyes are closing by themselves.

Your friend and sister in Christ,

Susanna

4

Tuesday, May 31

SOMEWHERE ALONG THE LINE, Stephen Kurtz had lost his belief in his ability to handle the curveballs that life threw at him. Oh, he believed that *Gott*'s power could see him through despite his many mistakes. But in the moment-by-moment of living through an experience? Lately, he wondered if he'd be able to hang onto his job, never mind his sanity. Poor Clancy's run-in with the barbed wire had been proof of that.

Like it or not, his grip on himself was slipping ... because he could not stop thinking about Susanna Miller.

The Bar K barn was a tidy, welcoming place. Josiah Keim had built the hands' bunkhouse on the floor above the horse stalls, next to a big room that, as well as their home, could be used for church once hay bales and equipment were moved out of it. The stairs from the bunkhouse descended inside the barn, instead of the outside of the building, which made sense in a climate that could be pretty unkind in the winter. Stephen ran a hand over Clancy's flank and was relieved to see that the cut was already healing.

"I'm sorry you have to put up with me, old friend," he murmured to the horse. "I'll do better, I promise. Once I work —this—out of my system."

"What's that?" Josiah Keim appeared in the doorway of the stall. "Were you talking to me?"

"Neh," Stephen said hastily. "I'm just checking that my mistake isn't causing Clancy here any pain."

Josiah nodded, his expert eye taking in what Stephen had just seen. "He'll be fine. You planning to head up the mountain today?"

"I had a word with the Eicher boys when I ran into them in the lower pastures yesterday. They said the herd was heading up Catcher Creek draw. I thought I might take a pack and a bedroll and spend a day or two checking calves."

Josiah frowned. "I'd wait on that. Catcher Creek is a long ways up, and I'm hearing some weather news that concerns me."

"On your new cell phone?" Stephen teased. Jonathan Keim was always ragging his father about the ancient flip phone he used for emergencies. A rancher in the high country couldn't be without something. An ancient phone could call for help as well as a new one, Josiah always replied.

The older man looked down his nose. "No. On the radio at the gas station, when I was filling the gas can for the generator. Appears the temp is going down near freezing this week."

Stephen stared. "It's almost June. Kind of late for a cold snap, ain't it? How soon?"

"Today maybe, but definitely by tonight. Kathryn and the girls will be disappointed. The garden was doing so well."

He exhaled, thinking about Catcher Creek. "That's a worry. The calves, I mean."

"Once it blows through, we'll all go up there and check on them. The mothers have seen enough weather that they'll hunker down and wait it out. The calves should follow their example, but there's always a few too stupid to do what they're told."

"I can relate," Stephen said with a smile. "All right. We'll *all* hunker down and wait it out. I've been wanting to take my saddle in for some repairs. Maybe today's the day. I hear there's a saddle maker in the valley name of John Cooper?"

"You heard right. But you'd do better to take it to Joshua Miller. He apprenticed with Cooper for a year and does a fine job for our folks."

Josiah drew a map on the back of the gas receipt, and Stephen walked out of the barn with him to get a look at the sky. Frowning, he took in the vast blue vault of heaven, looking exactly as it should on the last day of May. The air was a little cool, but it was early yet. The sun had cleared the peaks on the east side of the valley, but not by much. To the north, fluffy clouds were piling up, as though they'd tripped on the mountains and had bowled each other over.

"Freezing?" he asked nobody in particular. "Really?"

But Josiah was already out of earshot and didn't answer.

Stephen passed the weather report on to the other hands, and they buttoned up the barn, closing doors and checking feed and water in case the animals had to stay inside a day or two. They had a couple of cows in the home paddock who'd had a hard time calving, one because of age and another because of injury, and the calves still weren't up to a safe weight to turn them out. He directed the hands to bring them all into the barn. The horses ought to be fine in the home paddock; cold didn't bother them until it got below freezing, and Josiah hadn't indicated the thermometer would go that low. Then he and the hands packed up what they would need for a couple of days on the mountain once the squall had gone through.

Around eleven, the temperature had dropped noticeably, and he realized he'd better get a move on if he wanted to get that saddle over to Joshua Miller. If the man wasn't backed up with work, he might even be able to get the repairs done before the cold snap was over.

He tacked up Clancy and as he rode out, waved at Sylvia Keim, who was bringing in the washing they'd pegged out yesterday. Here, as in any community he'd ever lived in, Monday had been wash day. Sylvia was working pretty fast. She probably didn't want to dry everything again if it got frozen and then melted.

The Miller place was a fair distance away across the valley, and it took him the rest of the morning to ride there. The hay farm, Josiah had told him, had belonged to Sara Fischer Miller's family, but they'd died in a buggy accident, leaving her alone in the world. "And I mean *in the world*," Josiah had said gruffly. "She jumped the fence and was out of fellowship for years. When she came back, she put on an Amish dress and made up her mind to be baptized. Turned out Joshua was planning to jump the fence, too, and if it wasn't for hiring her as a nanny for the baby he found on the porch one morning, who knows where he would have ended up."

His stomach went cold. "The baby was ... his, I guess?"

"Yep," Josiah said.

Stephen didn't want to hear any more. He even gave serious thought to taking the saddle to this Cooper fellow, but he apparently lived all the way over by the lake. Stephen would never make it back if the weather decided to do something crazy.

Joshua was a cousin of Susanna's. Her father and his were brothers. How come he'd never heard about this baby business? And how had Joshua's wife Sara felt about becoming its mother? Where was the woman who had birthed it?

It was none of his business. Joshua was closer, and Amish, and a man should take his business to another Amishman if he could. Stephen buttoned his black wool jacket up to his chin. The temperature was really falling now, probably because a cutting north wind was blowing down the sides of the mountains. Why hadn't he pulled on his sheepskin coat, for goodness sake, instead of the barn jacket? Ach, well. Once he left the saddle with Joshua, he'd be riding home bareback at a pretty fast clip, and Clancy's body heat would keep him warm.

The farm was right where the gas receipt said it would be, with a neatly lettered sign hanging under the mailbox announcing FEED HAY—NO SUNDAY SALES. Something touched the back of his hand where he held Clancy's reins, light as a bit of dandelion fluff.

Snow. Even as he watched, the big snowflake melted on his skin. He hadn't brought gloves, either, or a scarf. He sighed. It was clear he wasn't done being stupid yet. The ride home was going to be uncomfortable—he'd best get his business over and start back, the sooner the better.

The house had probably been built in the seventies or eighties, and had recently been repainted the requisite light grey. The *Ordnung* here specified green or black trim for houses, so these folks had chosen green. The wraparound porch was welcoming, and a child's red wagon similar to the ones in Yoder's Variety Store lay abandoned close to the steps. He rode around back, to where a medium-sized shop with good-sized windows, also trimmed in green, faced the barn across the yard.

He looped Clancy's rein over the hitching rail and tried the shop door. Locked. "Hallo," he called. "I'm looking for Joshua Miller."

Silence greeted him.

He looked in the shop's window. A workbench was set up just below, with the tools of the harness maker's trade neatly put up in racks. Lengths of leather hung from iron hooks on the walls, and a half-finished saddle sat on a stand. A bookcase held what Stephen assumed were samples of patterns and styles that the client could choose from. The plank floor was neatly swept. It looked, in fact, as though the day's work hadn't yet begun. Either that, or the proprietor was away from home.

Stephen walked over to the house and knocked on the back door. "*Guder owed!* Anyone home?" The mudroom door was unlocked, but the inner door to the house wasn't. A piece of paper had been taped to the inside of its the four-light window.

GONE TO LIBBY. BACK THURSDAY.

"Oh," he said to the row of empty coat hooks and the quart jar of purple jam that sat on the bench under them. "That explains that." The question was, what should he do now? Go back to the ranch and try again another day? Or leave the saddle here in the mudroom with a note about what he needed done?

He closed the door behind him and stood on the porch, watching the snow come down with as much determination as if it were January. Good gravy—it was so thick that Clancy was merely a disgusted black outline. The horse nickered at him, as though to ask, *Why are we here and not in our safe, warm barn?*

If he left the saddle here without knowing how long the job was going to take, then he'd have to scrounge up an old one from Josiah in order to ride up the mountain after the storm. That was no way for a foreman to behave. *Neh*, better to ride home with it and do something smart the next time, like call over here instead of simply assuming a man would be in his shop working on a Tuesday.

Shaking his head at himself, Stephen made his way over to Clancy, who had lifted his head to look over Stephen's shoulder. He nickered and tossed his head. "Yes, we're going home. Sorry to give you a long ride for nothing, old man. Come on, we'll get a snack and some water for you before we head back."

He led the horse over to the barn, then hauled on the big sliding door just enough for Clancy to walk inside. Two draft horses and a cutting horse in one of the stalls lifted their heads and snorted in surprise at the intrusion, and several chickens scattered, flying up on a stack of hay bales to join two barn cats, who were staring down at him with suspicion. Stephen was just introducing himself to the Miller horses when both animals nickered together.

And now Stephen heard what his less sensitive ears had missed the first time—the sound of wheels on the gravel.

"There we go," he told Clancy. "They've probably had to turn around and come home. No *Englisch* taxi-van in its right mind would drive forty miles in weather like this."

He stepped to the door, pushing it wider to greet the couple. They'd stopped in the yard, maybe wondering how on earth the barn door had magically slid open. Odd. Usually the taxi-van picked people up right at the house.

With a wave, he stepped outside. "Hallo," he called. "Some weather, hey? Guess I'd better get moving and talk business another time."

Still no one inside responded. It was an ordinary family buggy, not one of the big multi-seat ones, but big enough for a couple and their baby. He approached it, smiling, vaguely aware that his boots were tamping down a good half inch of snow with each step. "Can I help you unhitch—"

He stopped, the snow falling like a veil, making it hard to see. It wasn't the Millers. It was a woman, and she seemed to be alone.

The buggy door slid open and a voice that he knew as well as his own said, "Stephen, what are you doing here? Don't you know there's a blizzard coming in?"

❧

THIS COULDN'T BE HAPPENING. SUSANNA STARED AT HIM through a whirling curtain of snow, wondering if her brain was making him up.

"I might ask you the same." Stephen stepped closer and gripped the side of the door. "This is no weather to be out in."

"The twins came down with the Eicher *Kind*'s cold, and Sara said she'd leave me a jar of her elderberry syrup." She pulled facts out of her brain. "She and Josh have gone to Libby. With Nathan. To the pediatrician."

"I know. They left a note. Back Thursday." He eyed the sky, which was like looking up into a snowdrift. "I hope they were able to stay ahead of this."

She glanced around the empty yard, rapidly filling with snow. "You couldn't have walked over here from the other side of the valley. Where's your buggy?"

"Don't have one. Just Clancy, and he's in the barn. I wanted to leave my saddle for repairs, but I guess I'd better hightail it back to Keims' before it gets worse. Oh, there's a jar of something purple in the mudroom. Is that your syrup?"

"*Ja*, that would be it. You're not going to ride home on the highway, are you?"

"Pretty hard to get back overland. What with the fences and all. Clancy's not much of a jumper."

"Ha ha, very funny." It was going to be dangerous. For both of them. "I need to get back, too. It's only going to get worse."

She jumped down and dashed into the mudroom, the snow touching her cheeks and forehead like icy fingertips. She grabbed the jar of syrup and closed the mudroom door firmly behind her. When she climbed back into the borrowed buggy, Stephen was leading a reluctant Clancy out of the barn. She waited just long enough for him to slide the barn door shut and mount up before she clicked her tongue to the horse and turned her back down the short lane.

When she stopped at the mouth of the lane to look both ways, Stephen drew up next to the driver's window. "I can't see a thing."

She didn't have a very *gut* feeling about this. "It's going to be a scary drive back, and this isn't even the county highway." Dutchman Road was pretty busy, though, under normal circumstances. Then she threw caution to the wind and blurted, "Stay with me, all right?"

He looked down at her, snow already piling on the brim of his hat. "Nervous?"

"Any sane person would be." Most sane people wouldn't be driving. Was it safe to make the left turn? All she could hear was the snow whispering all around them.

She clicked her tongue and Sal, the horse, started forward, Clancy moving ahead beside him.

With a roar and a horn that sounded like Gabriel's trumpet announcing the end of the world, a diesel rig came out of the whirling snow like a train and blasted past them. Susanna screamed as its wheels missed the horse's nose by a hand's breath and frightened her half out of her wits. Sal was going to rear—the buggy would overturn—

As though the same certainty had ignited in his mind, Stephen leaned over and grabbed Sal's harness. "Whoa," he said firmly. As he leaned back in the saddle, Clancy's reins in one hand, the other on the harness, Clancy responded like the professional he was and began to step backward.

"Gee, Sal," Susanna said, trying to sound soothing though her voice broke and tears had pooled in her eyes. "Gee up, that's it." Together, they got the buggy turned around in the mouth of the lane. When Stephen released the bridle she said, "Walk on, Sal," and to her enormous relief, the poor horse went willingly back to the yard.

Safe between the house and the barn once more, she palmed the cold tears of fright off her cheeks before she got out of the buggy a second time. "That's not going to work," she said thickly. "We can't drive in these conditions. We can't see them, and they can't see us."

"I thought diesel rigs weren't supposed to use Dutchman Road," Stephen said as he dismounted.

"The county highway must be blocked. Probably with stalled vehicles." She stroked the buggy horse's nose. "Hey, Sal. That was scary, wasn't it? You did just fine. I guess we'll put you in the barn for now, and wait it out."

Stephen led Clancy back to the barn doors, shoved them

open, and after he took his horse in, she turned Sal and backed the buggy in as well.

"I'll give you a hand unhitching her. There are a couple of empty stalls," he said. "They'll be more comfortable than we will, probably."

"I want to take good care of her. The Yoders loaned her and the buggy to me. Once they're settled, I'm going in the house."

"It's locked."

"I know where the spare key is."

How strange it felt, unhitching a horse together again. Walking her out of the slats. Currying both animals after he'd taken off Clancy's saddle and bridle. And finally, making sure their animals and the Miller horses watching them had all they needed in the hay and water department. It was as though the endless months since the last time had compressed to nothing, and her life was back to the way it had been.

But of course, nothing was the way it had been.

Stephen slid the heavy door closed behind them, and followed her across the yard. The snow was up past her ankles now, and she had to stamp her feet on the porch to shake it off. "It's really sticking."

"It can't last long. Hopefully it'll quit and melt before supper."

"Funny," she said, gazing out at it. The barn and shop had disappeared in the whirling maelstrom. "It's not the usual dry snow. It's heavy. Big, wet flakes."

"The state patrol is going to have a busy day," he predicted. "Isn't your cousin an EMT?"

"Adam and Zach both are. Sara—she lives here—used to be. And *ja*, I'm sure they've already been called out." She reached up to an abandoned swallow's nest in the angle made by the joists in the porch overhang, but her fingers couldn't quite reach over the rim. "Can you get the key? It's in here."

He had a couple of inches on her, and found the key easily. She well remembered his height, measured by the way her head fit on his shoulder, the way his arms went around her. She remembered how safe she'd felt in his embrace.

She'd never feel that way around him again.

❧ 5 ❧

MILLER HAY FARM

STEPHEN HANDED HER THE KEY, as though she were the hostess, and she let them in. The house was dead quiet—no generator running, no hiss of propane lanterns. No cheery sounds coming from the kitchen, no baby singing to himself and making sentences. It was as though the silence of the snow had come in with them.

"Is the stove still going?" He opened the flue, then the cast-iron door, and bent to check. "A few coals. I'll build it up, in case we have to hide out here for more than a couple of hours."

As jumpy and conflicted as she felt, a couple of hours was too many. But she didn't have much choice. Susanna shrugged out of her coat and hung it over one of the dining room chairs to dry. Her stomach gurgled and she realized it was long past noon. "I'm going to see what I can find for lunch. Are you hungry?"

"Starved."

This was just wrong, talking like a pair of polite strangers who'd met on the highway. Well, she supposed they were strangers, now. Nothing to talk about except the most mundane details of life while they waited to be free of each other's company.

With a sigh, she opened the fridge and took inventory. Sara was evidently a big believer in leftovers, for there were a couple of plastic tubs neatly stacked and full of food. That would do for supper if they were unlucky enough to be marooned here that long. She pulled out a loaf of homemade bread, some leftover roast beef, a block of the Zook brothers' cheese, and the mayonnaise and horseradish. She found enough jars neatly labeled TOMATO SOUP downstairs in the pantry to tell her it was a favorite in this household. Last summer's date told her they were likely a gift from the Circle M, to begin the young couple's housekeeping.

By the time the wood had caught and was producing the cheerful sound of crackling flames, the soup and sandwiches were ready. Stephen sat down at the table, carefully avoiding the chair belonging to the head of the household. After a silent grace that extended into just plain silence, he picked up his spoon and began to eat.

If politeness was the rule, it should include some conversation. Sometimes banalities were all you had.

"It seems funny to think of my cousin Joshua as the head of his own household," she said, breathing deeply at the bite of the horseradish. "He's the youngest of six, and was always a bit of a black sheep."

"I understand he was jumping the fence to go out when Sara was jumping back in." He, too, breathed deeply after the first pungent mouthful of his sandwich.

It was delicious.

"We weren't here then, but his sister Malena tells me that Nathan brought them together."

"The baby in the basket?" At her raised eyebrows, he said, "Josiah told me some of their story."

"Nathan's mother is an *Englisch* girl. Left to go to college. Malena says she told Josh she was never coming back, and to please not tell her parents. Which he did. They had a right to know they had a grandchild."

"Do they see Nathan?" He spooned hot soup into his mouth.

"I don't think so, though they live in Mountain Home. But Onkel Reuben and Aendi Naomi more than make up for it. There's no shortage of love at the Circle M. Not just for babies and animals, either. This past year has been one long case of wedding fever."

He smiled, just a twitch of his lips. "I look forward to meeting everyone. I've only been here a couple of weeks, and with turnout the big priority, there hasn't been much time for visiting outside of our—the east district."

Our district. Well, it was theirs, together with a lot of other people in the *Gmay*. Was he avoiding the use of that little word if it meant even the smallest connection with her?

With a mental sigh, she broke the silence again. "We moved here last winter. It was an adjustment. February was messy enough in New Mexico, but this was a whole other level of messy. The chinook winds, *nix?*"

"I've heard of them. They melt all the snow in a day, then the cold moves back in and freezes all the slush solid."

"It sure does." She could only talk about the weather for so long. "Anyway, we stayed at the Circle M after we arrived, and at Christmas, some of Aendi Rachel's relatives from Prince Edward Island came for Rebecca and Noah's wedding."

"That must've been a houseful."

"It was. We spilled over into Daniel and Lovina's house—

that's my oldest cousin and his wife. And on the heels of the wedding came Zach's engagement to Ruby Wengerd, the bishop's daughter. Zach is—" She counted. "The third son."

"Does the bishop have a big family?"

Most Amish did. Was he just pulling questions out of thin air? "I think Ruby is the only one left at home. The others are married and raising their own families."

"The bishop's a rancher?"

"I don't think so. He has a big farm, though, so he grows hay, and has a few head of cattle, and I think he's kind of mechanical, too."

"Repairs and conversions and such?"

"Maybe. One of the men on the east side does that. Converts electric machines to hydraulic. The *Ordnung* here allows it." Some of the plainer churches didn't.

Stephen laid his spoon in his empty bowl. "Any more soup?"

"*Ja*, enough for another bowl."

To her surprise, he poured half of the remaining soup in his bowl, and handed the pot to her. "Finish the rest."

"But—"

He shook his head. "This will fill me up."

That was nice of him. She emptied the pot, and enjoyed the last spoonfuls of soup, making a mental note to ask for the recipe the next time she went to the Circle M.

He cocked an eye at the window. "Is it my imagination, or is it getting darker?"

Now that he mentioned it, the light in the room had faded some. Not enough for her to light the Coleman chandelier, but enough to notice. She collected their plates and bowls, and ran water into the sink. While it filled, she gazed out the back window, which overlooked the barn opposite and the shop on the right side of the yard.

"I think you're right. So much for a long summer evening. There's a foot of snow now. Look, up to the bottom rail of the corral. We'll know we're in trouble when it gets to the fourth bar."

He didn't laugh as he joined her to peer out the window. "Best keep an eye on that for a ruler—this isn't giving me a *gut* feeling about letting up anytime soon." He stepped away, clearly objecting to sharing a window with her, too. "I wonder what the forecast is?"

"Look on your phone," she suggested.

He shook his head. "I was only running an errand. I left it in the barn for Josiah to put on the charger with the others when he started the generator."

An errand of sixteen miles round trip with no phone? But it was not her place to say that out loud, and anyway, he'd obviously figured out it hadn't been the wisest thing to do. In ranch country, being able to communicate over its vast spaces was a necessity. She went back to the sink and started the dishes.

"Where's *your* phone?" he asked from the stove in the living room, where he was putting in another piece of wood.

"I don't have one. The boys do, but I'm not out riding fence with them, or roaming for miles on an allotment, so I just use the Inn's phone if I need to deal with the laundry people or ask Sara for elderberry syrup." She sighed. "Poor Gracie and Benny. At this rate, they'll have to settle for something from that funny little drugstore in town. The pharmacist looks like a garden gnome and hides in the back until you ring the bell."

"*Ein Erdgeischt?* Complete with tall red hat?"

"I'm sure he wears one for Christmas."

Was that a chuckle? But he'd closed the stove door on the sound, so she couldn't be certain. She had to be careful. The jokes funny only to them paved a dangerous path, just like good intentions.

"Well, just in case I'm here longer than I want to be, I'll get some wood in."

Longer than *he* wanted to be? Alone with her? Hurt prickled through her chest, but all she said was, "The shed's on the near side of the barn, on the left."

"I saw it."

He found a pair of work gloves in the mudroom, and as she rinsed the dishes, she watched him make a path from the kitchen door across the yard, up to his knees in heavy snow. There was no crust on it, of course, so walking was difficult whether he slogged through it or picked up his feet to make single holes with each step. Coming back with a big armload of wood was even more difficult, because he had to crane his head around his high, heavy burden to try to stay in the path he'd made.

The footprints closest to the porch steps were already filling, their outlines blurred.

She held open the door as he stamped snow off his boots and the legs of his jeans, then staggered in with the load of wood. His arms gave out and he dumped the entire load in the woodbox with a crash. They landed neatly, all facing the same way. Of course they did. No higgledy-piggledy mess with bark all over the floor for Stephen. She always had to sweep up after herself when she brought in wood.

"I'd better fetch more," he said, heading for the door. "No telling how much snow we'll get, or whether I'll be able to find the shed if it gets worse."

That sounded a bit extreme, she thought as she dried their dishes. Stephen wasn't usually a pessimist. Maybe his time away had been more difficult than she knew.

Once the dishes were done, she put a pot of coffee on and in the fridge found a plastic bin full of neat squares of cake. Applesauce spice cake with caramel frosting—definitely a bright spot in a very strange afternoon.

When she heard his boots on the porch, she swung the door open and he brought in the second load of wood. After depositing it in the woodbox, he didn't stop there. "One more for the back door."

How long did he think the storm would last? It would take two days to get through what was inside now. But before she could ask, he plunged back into the whirling whiteness, following the trail he'd made. The barn and shop were both invisible.

She took a plate of cake and two cups of coffee—hoping he still took his black—into the living room and settled on the sofa to wait. Sara's mother's engagement clock ticked on its shelf in the *Eck*. Ten minutes. Fifteen.

A few minutes more, and she set her half-finished mug down and went to the kitchen window. Twenty minutes was far too long. Had something happened to him? Had the trail been obliterated and he was out there somewhere, wandering in this nightmare of swirling snow?

Lieber Gott, let him be all right. Protect and keep him. Bring him back to me.

Five more agonizing minutes crawled by. And then something moved like a shadow, and a gray form emerged out of the snow. Susanna's breath went out of her in a rush, and her hands shook as she opened the kitchen door. She dragged cold air into her lungs as he dumped the heavy armload of wood in the empty iron rack just outside the door.

"I was getting worried," she managed.

He stamped snow off his boots and after he brushed an inch or so off his hat, smacked his coat and pants with it. Then he came inside and she closed the door behind him.

"I figured I should check on the animals and make sure they all had feed and water for the morning as well. If this doesn't let up, it will be harder to find my way out there."

"Surely it won't go on that long."

He shrugged out of his coat and hung it over the chair next to hers, and toed off his boots. "No telling. Best to be prepared for the worst, and not risk someone else's animals."

"They likely had a neighbor coming to look after them, but at this rate, whoever it is won't be able to drive a buggy, or even find the farm. It's a whiteout."

"That it is. Lucky we were here. Hey, is that cake?"

"Applesauce spice. If your coffee is cold, I can heat it up."

He took a sip. "*Neh*, it's fine." He helped himself to a piece of cake and settled on the sofa where she had been sitting. "Food, coffee, and cake. I guess there are worse ways to be snowbound."

He omitted any mention of his company, or who had prepared the food. She took a piece of cake and settled in the armchair at an angle to the sofa, watching the flames dance in the stove. The first bite of cake was heaven on her tongue. "If I'd left just fifteen minutes later, I'd have been stuck on the road trying not to be killed by another diesel rig."

"Maybe *Gott*'s hand was guiding both of us. I sure hope no one else is out there—Amish or *Englisch*."

"How can the EMT van drive in this if someone does get stuck?"

"I don't know. I haven't heard the plow, either. They probably put it away for the season." He sipped his coffee, gazing at the fire. "Maybe we should be prepared for visitors. You know, people leaving their buggies or cars and walking to find shelter."

"This house is closer to the road than some," she agreed. "But I don't know how visible it is—all our homes are grey."

All the same, she'd better find out where Sara kept the blankets. "They have four guest rooms, so if someone does have to spend the night, they can."

"Like us." For the first time, his gaze found hers deliberately. "Is Rachel going to be worried if you don't come home?"

"She's probably worried now, and watching the highway. I need to call. They must have a cell phone here."

But a search of all the places the phone might be— including Josh and Sara's bedroom—turned out to be fruitless. "They've taken it with them," Susanna sighed, snagging another piece of cake on the way back to the armchair. "Poor Mamm. I hope she doesn't send the boys out to look for me."

"They know you have the sense to find somewhere to wait it out."

If that was a compliment, she'd nearly missed it.

He went to the kitchen for the coffee pot, and refilled her mug without being asked. Then he filled his own while she added cream from the little ceramic creamer she'd put on the coffee table. When he came back, he said casually, "How are your brothers doing?"

Okay, not strangers. More like acquaintances.

"They're well. Gideon and Seth signed on as hands on the Circle M, since Joshua is here now and Adam is building his home with Noah King." She huffed a laugh. "We were supposed to have a barn raising once turnout was done. I wonder if it will happen now?"

"Impossible to say. I heard about a barn raising, but Josiah didn't bring it up when I said I'd spend a few days up on the allotment checking calves."

"Probably because healthy calves are his income, and our barn isn't."

Still, she would have missed him. Wondered why he wasn't there. Worried and fretted ... and all for nothing, because of course he had to put his employer's calves first. Which made her wonder how the calves were going to get through this.

"And Tobias?" he asked.

"It's almost a full-time job managing the twins. He's picking up work where he can, but he doesn't feel right signing on with a ranch full time. Not when he couldn't live there and be where he was needed. So he helps Mamm with the Inn, and he's become friendly with the owner of the feed store across the highway. I think the man might have grown up Amish, though he isn't now. He might hire Tobias because of how busy it is in the summer."

"A rancher, working at a feed store? That doesn't sound like Tobias."

"How would you know?" came out of her mouth before her brain knew what it was up to. "Things can change, I mean," she amended, less harshly. "He had planned to work full time at the Inn, but then Luke came along, and it seems right that a married couple should work there together. Mamm has always wanted it to be more like a home than a hotel."

"I don't know Luke. What's his story?"

She gave him the bare outlines—his lost family, the years of solitude drifting from job to job, and the care of his Heavenly

Father that had brought both him and Mamm back to this valley again, full circle.

"And how do you all feel about your *mamm* remarrying?"

She had to be honest, and it made her uncomfortable to confess it. She looked into her mug and mumbled, "I wasn't very nice to him."

"I can't believe that. Why not?"

Still not looking up, she said, "I thought she'd been carrying a torch for him the whole time she was married to Dat. I thought she was being unfaithful in her heart."

The shocked silence made her raise her eyes. And yes, he was staring at her with just such an expression. "Wow," he said. "Did you tell her that?"

"You know me," she said on a sigh. "In through the brain, out through the mouth."

You know me. Why had she said that? He didn't know her. Not anymore.

She plowed on. "In the end it was Luke himself who made me see it differently. You see, Dat knew about the two of them. All those years they were married, he knew. And loved her anyway. If Dat was willing to wait for her to love him, then what business was it of mine if Luke came a-courting after he was gone?"

"And now they're making wedding plans."

"I'm going to enjoy every minute." She could feel her shoulders relaxing. "It will be small—just the families here. Luke plans to write to his sisters, so they might come. I predict a lot of weddings on the Circle M this winter, too."

"The bishop will be a busy man."

"Especially when his daughter is one of the brides."

He moved restlessly, and got up to check the stove. It was burning just fine, and she could see from where she sat that the wood had a while yet before it needed to be replenished. He took his empty mug out to the kitchen and put it in the sink.

She should have expected he wouldn't sit still for talk of weddings. Any second now he'd grab his coat and plunge out into the snow for more firewood, just to get away.

Instead, he went to the front door and looked through the two-light window in it, his head cocked like that of a curious robin.

"What is it?" she asked, putting down her own empty mug.

"Funny—when we were eating lunch, and it seemed to get dark, the streetlights came on. They're out now."

She couldn't see the power poles, but she should have been able to see the glow. "The power's out."

It wouldn't matter to the Amish community, because they didn't live on the grid. But it might matter very much to their *Englisch* neighbors, especially if the temperature fell any lower.

6

STEPHEN THOUGHT he might come right out of his skin. Not just because he was an outdoorsman, and rarely spent much time in the house. Even in winter, there was always some job or repair that needed to be done in the barn, or there was something to fabricate in the shop, or a man could tidy up or move equipment if all else failed. But being forced to sit in a room making conversation with the woman he'd once wanted to marry was about the finest torture *der Herr* could devise.

It was pretty clear that while *Gott* might be up to something beyond Stephen's understanding, Susanna hadn't forgiven him for leaving the Four Winds Ranch. He'd had no choice but to go. And there were no words to tell her why. So because he wouldn't lie to her, he'd simply closed his mouth, packed his things, and ridden away, knowing that he had deliberately broken something beautiful that could not be repaired.

His only consolation had been that she'd soon be safely married, and he could pick up and move on with his life.

So much for consolation.

She put the cake they hadn't eaten back in the plastic tub

with an air of virtuous sacrifice, and returned it to the refrigerator. Then she curled up in the armchair to gaze at the fire, looking so sweet and soft it took all he had to put the coffee table between them and sit his sorry self down on the far end of the sofa. How easy it would be to scoop her out of the chair and settle her in his lap! To kiss her senseless—taste the caramel frosting on her lips—and when they were both breathless, to beg her to forgive him. Ask her if there was any chance the broken could be mended.

Get thee behind me, Stephen. He closed his hands, which had opened as though they wanted to reach for her. That was never going to happen. She deserved better than a fool who could make such a colossal mistake. He would make sure to stay out of the way so that she could have the very best *Gott* had in store for her.

"So," she said, still gazing into the fire, "how are your family? Have you heard from them lately?" She looked over at him. "We enjoyed that time your parents and youngest sisters came to New Mexico for Thanksgiving."

Two Thanksgivings ago. When he and Susanna were feeling the sparkles of attraction and trying not to let anyone know it—including each other.

Conversation, he told himself. Not memories. Memories were dangerous.

"I don't think a letter has had time to find me here, but the last one I had said that they were both well, and Christie had had twins, much to her dismay and Conrad's delight."

Susanna smiled as though she remembered Tobias feeling the same. "How many do they have now?"

"Five, all under seven. They're still in Charm, along with Mamm and Dat, and so is my brother Eldon and my younger sister Miriam. Both married. Eldon has one boy with another baby on the way, and Miriam is expecting her first."

"And the girls? We had so much fun teaching them to ride a cutting horse."

"Mamm says they're thriving, but since they moved up to Berlin, they don't see them quite as often. They sure won't get much practice riding there—no cutting horses. No riding on any kind of horse. The bishops have strong feelings about women riding astride. And men, for that matter."

"What took them up there?"

She'd got along well with his sisters. Keturah was the same age as Susanna, Dinah two years younger. Keturah had the eyes of a hawk, and it had been she who had informed him that Susanna had a crush on him. Until that moment, he'd thought he was paddling that canoe alone.

Susanna was watching him now, probably wondering why he was taking so long to answer. "There's an old *Englisch* lady running a bed and breakfast in this big old Victorian house. Aendi Elsie works in the kitchen, and when the two chambermaids left to get married, she suggested the girls. They live onsite, the pay is generous, and since it's only four miles away, apparently they're enjoying the flirting in two groups of *Youngie*, not just one."

Susanna laughed. "I heard the crowds at singing are pretty big in Ohio."

"*Ja*, they are. I left when I was sixteen to go out to Colorado, but I remember the size of the few singings I got to."

"As opposed to the Ventana Valley, where I think we *Youngie* numbered fourteen when the *Gmay* was at its largest."

"Small, but mighty."

"And now gone," she said wistfully. "I would have stayed on

the ranch. But while we could have kept it going as a business, you can't live without the *Gmay*, can you?"

He had, briefly. And he didn't want to do it again. "*Neh*, we can't. It's more than having help when you need it, and neighbors with the same goals and beliefs in life. It's the fellowship. The spirit of the church. If you don't have that, it's hard for your soul to thrive."

She was quiet for a moment. "Sounds like the voice of experience."

He'd let his feelings run away with him, and now he had to backtrack. "I don't think you'll find too many of our people who feel differently."

"True, but not many of them would put it that way. Did something happen, Stephen?"

He couldn't say yes, and to say no would be a lie. So he said, "Does something need to happen, to appreciate our ways?"

"*Neh* ... but ..."

He had to tell her something, so a partial truth would have to do.

"Part of the reason I left Holmes County was because I was on *Rumspringe*. Headstrong, stubborn, and willing to indulge in more than a few bad habits. Desperate for the wide open spaces instead of the tidy farms and high expectations of home. I was just lucky to wind up on the ranch near Monte Vista, where I lived with the Amish foreman and his family. I think both families saved me from jumping the fence altogether ... and I learned how to do the work I came to love."

"I remember you telling me about them. The Schrocks had the ranch?"

"*Ja*. I'm still—" But he couldn't finish. *I'm still in contact with them*. Why had he brought them up? Why did this conversation keep veering onto the rocks of his poor decisions instead of sailing placidly along on polite exchanges of news? How did other people manage conversation for more than two minutes?

But then, he and Susanna had once talked for hours. About everything—their deepest hopes and dreams, their fears, their mistakes. Before.

Now it was After, and he had to get used to the fact that everything was different.

She stirred in the armchair. "We should turn on a light. Not just because it's really dim in here, but someone might be walking to find help and they might see it."

"*Gut* idea."

The living room windows faced Dutchman Road, which he couldn't see in the whirling white, and looked across the intervening hay field, which he couldn't see, either. After a look out the kitchen door, he pulled the pole lamp on its propane-tank base over to the front window and lit it, then turned it down so it didn't blind both of them on the high setting. Just as well they had a little light. A dim room with a fire going was all too conducive to confidences.

He wasn't prepared for those. Would never be.

But there was a subject that had to be brought up. "We should think about what we're going to do if the snow doesn't stop before dark."

Tucked up in her chair, she'd been gazing at the snow, and now her startled gaze swung to meet his. "You don't think it will?"

He lifted one shoulder in a shrug. "Even if it does, I looked out just now and saw it's up to the second rail on that fence. We won't get a horse or a buggy out until it melts."

"The plow will come through. It has to."

"Sure, after it gets done clearing all the streets in town. The folks staying at the Inn might be able to get in and out, but I'm thinking this side of the valley is not exactly a priority."

"The Inn." She covered her lips with her fingertips. "Poor Mamm. Only four of the fishermen were scheduled to leave this morning. That leaves six guests and the twins she still has to manage alone."

"Alone?"

She nodded. "Gid and Seth will be at work. Tobias was doing a feed delivery to someone on the east side. I hope everyone is all right."

"They would all have gone in and found shelter," he said, trying to be reassuring. "Just like you did." Her younger brothers would probably be fine at the Circle M. But depending on where Tobias had to deliver the feed, there were some pretty lonely stretches of road out that way, between ranches.

Maybe he'd better not bring that up.

"I'm worried about Tobias," she said, in that uncanny way she had of picking up on his thoughts.

"Will your worrying help him?"

Her face scrunched into something between a frown and a smile. "Of course not."

"Then don't waste your energy on it. When you can't do anything—"

"—do what you can," she finished for him.

With a smile, he said, "Tobias told me that once, when I was *verhuddelt* about something. Said his father taught him."

"I guess I'd better remember a few more of Dat's little sayings," she said on a sigh. "Honestly, if I look out that window any more, the snow will drive me crazy."

"I don't like driving a buggy in it," he agreed. "Your eyes go everywhere and you get all disoriented."

A silence fell. Then she stirred.

"So. Getting back to what happens when it gets dark, I don't see we have much choice but to stay put. We can't leave —we've already proven that. No one is coming to look for us."

"They'll all assume each of us went somewhere to wait it out."

"I hope they assume that," she said, nibbling a corner of her upper lip. "I hope Mamm doesn't think I'm upside down in a ditch somewhere."

He must not look at her lips.

"And now you're worrying about what Rachel is worrying about."

At least he'd made her laugh at herself. "You're right," she said. "Well, all the beds are made up, so I suppose we can eat some of the leftovers and spend the night. Then dig ourselves out in the morning."

"And hope to goodness no one hears about it," he said. "I promise not to tell if you don't."

She stared at him.

He tried to elaborate. "You know, the Amish grapevine. If it gets out that we spent the night alone together, the gossip will be fierce."

"We are not spending the night together!"

"You know that, and I know that, but the fact is, if we have to stay overnight and someone finds out, it will be all over the valley in minutes."

She pushed herself upright in the armchair, her relaxed posture transformed by a spine as rigid as a poker. "You say that as though—as though there was any possibility in the *world* we might do something worth gossiping about."

Did she have to put it like that? "People don't know. All they'll see is two *Youngie* who are new to the valley, who had ... a history together, who spent the night alone. They'll assume the worst."

"They will not!" If it were possible, she became even more rigid. "I haven't said a word to anyone here about my *history*. It certainly wasn't anything to brag about."

Her words punched him in the gut. The tone of disdain took his breath. Is that what she thought? That those moments that had been so precious to him, that had sustained him in his darkest moments even though they could never be repeated ... they were *nothing to brag about*?

When had she learned to be so cruel?

"People might know you were our foreman in New Mexico, but no one except the family knows there was ..." She paused, clearly searching for more words to hurt him with. "Anything more. Or nothing more, as it turned out."

A man could only be poked with a sharp stick so many times before he poked back. "So if you were snowed in with say, Dave Yoder, people would just nod and smile and go about their business?"

"Dave Yoder?" she repeated incredulously. "What does he have to do with anything?"

"You tell me. Or did you make a little *history* when you went home with him after singing?"

"That is none of your business." She stuck her nose in the air and looked away.

"So you did," he said. "If he was the guy in here with you, would you be sitting on the other side of the room like you are now? Or would you be cuddled up on this sofa, and telling people you were just trying to stay warm?"

If looks could kill, he'd be a smoking spot on the cushions. "*First*, I would not be cuddling up anywhere on this planet with Dave Yoder. And *second*, I am perfectly capable of building a fire in a stove if I need one. I don't need some judgmental stick in the mud to do it for me."

That shocked a laugh out of him. "Is that what he is? Or did you mean me?"

"I meant him," she snapped. "You're a lot of things, but judgmental isn't one of them. Do you know he actually thought Cora Swarey was being *prideful* when she sent out 'After the Fire' with her wedding invitations?"

"He told you that?"

"He certainly did. And when I suggested that maybe it was so people could learn the song and sing it after the wedding, he didn't believe me."

"Ouch. So ... will you be seeing him again?"

The iron might be melting out of her spine, but now she had her arms crossed over her chest. "I don't know. I'd have to eat a whole cake before a date to make myself sweet enough for that one—and I already have enough trouble with my weight."

He tried not to laugh at Dave's expense, but what came out was a muffled snort. "It could be worth making yourself sick— I mean, sweet. He and Calvin have partnerships in the store."

She leveled a look at him. "Are they worth the price of dating Dave? Or, heaven forbid, having Calvin as a brother-in-law?"

He made a horrified face. "Please don't make that sacrifice. I beg you."

"All right." She settled more comfortably into the chair. "But only because you begged."

Little did she know he'd been completely serious. "Sharon and Bethany Keim predicted right in front of me that Dave would ask if he could give you a ride home. If not last Sunday, then certainly the next. Apparently he's asked out every *Maedshe* in the *Gmay*."

"And now he's picking off the new girls one by one?"

He shook his head in mock admiration. "You have to admire his guts, if not his wisdom."

"All the girls talk about him. He has no idea."

"Well, you know what they say. There's someone for everyone. Even Dave."

"I hope so. Then the rest of us will be safe." After a moment, she said more seriously, "To be honest, Stephen, after a storm like this I'm pretty sure people will be so glad to see their loved ones safe and sound that reputations and propriety won't come up. If they do, I believe it would say more about the spirit of that person than the morals of whoever had to take shelter."

"Let's hope you're right. Because if I thought my being here would put you in a compromising situation, I'd head out and sleep in the barn. Once I found it."

She made a disbelieving noise in her throat. "If a fuss like that kicked up, sleeping in the barn wouldn't help. You'd have to almost die of exposure walking home for some people to be satisfied. I don't think there are too many folks like that in the Siksika Valley. People here tend to think the best of one another, don't you find?"

"I've been around more cows than people since I moved here, but at least on the Bar K, I can say that's true."

"I know it is on the Circle M. And at the Inn."

So there was something he didn't have to worry about. The people closest to them, whose opinions meant the most, would fall on their necks rejoicing when they returned safely. As for anyone else's opinion, well, the only one he cared about was that of *der Herr*.

Who seemed to have engineered this whole impossible situation.

7

THE WILD ROSE AMISH INN

4:40 p.m.

"Susanna should have been back hours ago." Rachel Miller paced from the guest dining room through the kitchen to the family parlor and back again. "What if she got stranded on the highway? What if the buggy got hit by a car and she's lying in a ditch, unconscious?"

"Mammi, you're scaring me." Gracie's little voice, hoarse and fretful, came from the sofa. She and Benny were tucked up under a quilt sipping hot lemonade with apple cider vinegar and dollops of honey in the absence of the elderberry syrup that had taken Susanna on her errand.

The weather had been perfect when she'd left this morning. It had turned within the hour, though, and become a blizzard the likes of which Rachel hadn't seen since she was a child.

"I have to say, you're kind of scaring me, too," one of the burly fishermen said, looking up from the chess board in the keeping room, where he was playing his companion. "If I thought I could get my truck down the highway, I'd go look for her."

"Don't even think about it," Sandra, one of the two lady anglers, said. "No truck can get through three feet of snow, and it's still coming down."

"We'll be considering ice fishing next," Merrill offered. "Thermometer says nineteen degrees."

"She was going to Josh and Sarah's," Rachel said fretfully. "I'll try them again."

The cell phone, which usually lived in the center drawer of the office desk in her bedroom, hadn't left her pocket since the snow began. She dialed the hay farm's number, and to her immense relief, it went through.

"Sara, thank goodness. I've been trying for hours. It's Aendi Rachel. Is Susanna there with you?"

A pause. "Here with us? Aendi, we're in Libby. We came down to take Nathan to the pediatrician for his shots. They don't let us have the phone on at the clinic, and then I forgot to turn it on when we left."

All the air went out of Rachel's body and she sat suddenly on one of the dining room chairs. "You're in *Libby*?"

"*Ja*. I left the elderberry syrup in the mud room for Susanna. Aendi, we're hearing about an awful storm up there. It's snowing here, but only sprinkles. Are you folks all right?"

"We're fine here at the Inn. But Susanna would have got to the hay farm just as it started, and we haven't heard from her. I've been calling and calling."

"I'm so sorry. It was my mistake. We're at a B&B now, and were planning to come home tomorrow, but Jimmy says the highway's closed. He and his taxi-van are here, too."

"It's three feet deep and no sign of stopping, so I'm not surprised." She took a breath and tried to calm herself. No point in worrying Sara and Joshua when they were so far away. "I'm sure Susanna took shelter at your place and didn't try to come back here."

"I'm sure she did," Sara said in a soothing tone. "There is lots of food in the fridge, and she knows where we keep the key. She'll be fine, Aendi. Don't you worry. Are you alone?"

Rachel laughed, only slightly out of control. "*Neh*, I have six guests and two *kranke Kinner* with me. Gideon and Seth were at the Circle M, so I'm not worried about them. Tobias was out on a delivery, but there are any number of Amish places along the way where he could take shelter. It's only Susanna I'm not certain of."

"*Der Herr* will keep her," Sara said with a confidence Rachel wished she could recover. "We'll pray for her."

"And we'll pray for you three, and Jerry. Tell him to drive safely once they open the highway."

"I'm sure I won't be able to help it," Sara said with a laugh. "Good-bye, Aendi. Breathe."

It was *gut* advice.

"Not there?" the burly fisherman asked. Carson, his name was.

"No, Sara had the phone and they're both in Libby with the baby. I'm going to call the Circle M again. They might have heard something by now."

Reuben picked up on the first ring. He, too, had been carrying the phone in his pocket. "Circle M Ranch."

"Reuben, it's Rachel."

"We haven't heard from her. Your boys have come in. Naomi scolded them about tracking snow into her kitchen, and then she gave them a big hug and a piece of cake."

A little of the fear in her heart melted. "I just spoke with Sara down in Libby. Jimmy the taxi-van driver says the highway is closed, so she and Joshua may be staying longer than overnight."

"I thought that might happen. She hasn't heard from Susanna?"

"*Neh*. Susanna didn't take a phone, though, so she wouldn't have. I'm doing my best not to worry, but it's difficult. Of course *mei Dochsder* would stay put. Sara says there is plenty of food, and she knows where the key is."

"I'm sure she's safe and warm," Reuben said in the same soothing tone he'd used the first time she'd called.

"Have you heard from your Adam and Zach?"

"Not in a couple of hours, but then, we didn't expect to. Your friend Brock Madison from the Rocking Diamond called over and said there were cars stranded up and down the main roads in the valley. Two dozen at least, the news report said, and a quarter of those are in the ditch being slowly buried. I expect the volunteer fire department is busy trying to get people to safety. Some may have to wait it out in their cars if the emergency crews can't get to them."

Your friend Brock Madison. If the situation hadn't been so worrisome, Rachel would have rolled her eyes at Reuben's dry humor. Splashing half a pot of coffee on the wealthy *Englisch* man, as she'd accidentally done a few months ago, had not been her most shining moment. "I suppose folks in cars would be warm enough with the heater going."

Reuben made a noise in his throat. "That's not what Brock says. Even if they had enough gas to keep the engine running, if the snow gets deep enough, the exhaust system can back up into the car and asphyxiate them."

"Reuben, do not tell me things like that right now."

"Susanna isn't in a car, Rachel. And I'm very glad Joshua

and Sara aren't, either. *Dei Dochsder* is almost certainly reading a book with a fire going in the stove."

"I hope so," Rachel said on a sigh. "The hand of *Gott* will protect her."

"For sure and certain. If I hear anything, I'll call. And you do likewise."

"I will." It took all Rachel's strength to break the tenuous connection with her brother-in-law's comforting voice.

The fisherman who was reading one of Marlon's books on tying flies looked up. "No news?"

"No. But my boys are safe at the house, and my brother-in-law is certain Susanna is at the hay farm." She tried to pull herself together. "Since it's unlikely any of the restaurants in town are still open, I'll get busy making some dinner for us all."

"I'll help," Sandra said.

"Can I do anything for the little ones?" Carson asked. "They can play games on my phone if they want."

Rachel closed her lips briefly on an exclamation of dismay. "No, but thank you for the offer. I'm hoping that once they have a little to eat, they'll go to sleep."

"No, we won't," Benny croaked from the family parlor, peering over the quilt. "I want to play a game on his phone."

"If you're well enough for that, you're well enough to do your spelling words," Rachel informed him.

Benny ducked under the quilt like a spooked rabbit bolting into the grass. School had ended when the first hay crop came off a few days ago, but much to Benny's disgust, his father saw no reason why his children couldn't keep up with at least one or two new words each week until September.

She squashed a twinge of concern about Tobias. If worse came to worst, he could unhitch the horse from the delivery wagon and ride it bareback to safety. The animal had better clearance in the snow.

As Sandra set the table and Rachel gathered some ingredients that she could combine with yesterday's leftovers to make dinner for eight, she glanced out the window over the sink. She couldn't even see the chicken coop, which was not fifteen feet from the house.

Suddenly she needed to hear an even dearer voice. As far as she was concerned, this was enough of an emergency to satisfy the bishop. She took the phone with her into her bedroom and closed the door.

"Zook Dairy and Catering."

She blinked. "Hezekiah, since when did you and Willard take up catering?"

"Since lunch. It was Luke's idea. Want to talk to him?"

"*Ja, bidde.*"

"No trouble?"

"I don't know yet. We think Susanna is at the hay farm, and I'm hoping Tobias found somewhere safe before it got too bad."

"And the boys?"

"At the Circle M."

"*Gut.* Well, here's Luke."

"Hallo, *mei Liebe. Bischt du* okay?"

For some silly reason, her eyes filled with tears at the endearment. "I'm all right." She cleared her throat and told him about her *Kinner*, both what she feared and the news of a moment ago that had brought relief.

Luke, seasoned cowboy that he was, knew what to fear as well as she did. "Remember the blizzard when we were *Kinner*? Aendi Annie King had to climb out the second story window because the drifts were up to the eaves."

"She is probably telling that story to the Kings at this very moment, and assuring them this is nothing in comparison."

"Some day we'll have our own story to tell."

"If I knew Susanna and Tobias were safe, I'd be able to look forward to that day."

He was silent a moment. "We have every reason to believe they are. One of them being our faith that *der Herr* will care for His children."

"I know. I'm doing my best to be brave, for Gracie and Benny's sake, but also for our guests. The last thing they need in this strange experience is to see their hostess breaking down."

"I bet they've never been so thankful to be in a place that doesn't depend on electricity," Luke said, a smile in his voice.

"One of the fishermen told me that the power is out all through the valley. People are depending on their phones for now, but when the phones run down, everyone will be in the dark."

"In more ways than one. Better not tell Zeke and Willard that. They'll be asking a dollar a minute for *Englisch* folks to charge their phones in the barn." He paused. "If they can find it."

"Speaking of barns, I'm having doubts our barn raising is going to happen when we hoped."

"You never know. This could all melt as fast as it came." After a moment, he said, "Rachel, tell me true. Do you want me to go over to the hay farm and make sure Susanna is there and all right?"

She leaped off the bed. "*Neh!* Don't you dare!"

"Will has snowshoes," he said. "I could—"

"Luke, I could not bear to lose you so soon after we've

found each other. Promise me you won't go out. It's not safe. She's perfectly fine, I'm sure of it."

"All right," he said quietly after a moment. "I promise."

Even as she let out a breath of relief, her heart swelled a little more with love at his willingness to put himself at risk for Susanna. Not so many days ago, they had been at loggerheads —to the point that each would have been happy to send the other into a worse blizzard than this.

"But I love you for offering," she whispered.

"*Ich liebe dich*, Rachel. We will be praying together for Susanna and Tobias."

"I love you, too. Good-bye for now."

And as she made her way back to the kitchen, it was almost as though both Luke and *der Herr* walked beside her, comforting in their presence, both certain that everything would be all right.

8

MILLER HAY FARM

6:10 p.m.

THERE MIGHT HAVE BEEN a long summer evening happening somewhere, but in the Siksika Valley, the low, dark clouds and snow had turned everything to twilight. There were two Coleman pole lamps, the other in the kitchen so Susanna could see to make dinner. He set the table for two, stoked up the woodstove once more, and checked to make sure there was gas in the generator in the little shed at one end of the back porch, in case it might be needed.

"I found what looks like elk sausage and chile casserole," Susanna said over her shoulder when he came in, blowing on his hands. "Sara must have got the recipe from Aendi Naomi, who got it from Mamm."

"Sounds *wunderbaar.*"

She slid the casserole pan into the gas stove to heat, and when she took the potato peeler from a drawer, he indicated the potatoes on the counter. "I'll do those."

She handed it to him handle first, so that no part of their fingers would touch. But the peeler was new and sharp, and as he took it, it nicked her forefinger. "Mmph!" She put the side of her finger in her mouth, and hurried over to get a tissue. "That was silly of me."

"I'll get a Band-Aid strip."

"Bathroom," she said around her finger.

He found a box in the medicine cabinet and peeled the wrappings off a bandage, then returned to the kitchen.

"I can do it," she said.

"I know. Here. Let me." He took her hand and dabbed at the bleeding cut with the tissue, then wrapped the bandage expertly around her finger. Her hand was warm. Soft. And, he realized with a little jolt, this was the first time he had touched her in almost a year.

He wanted to hold that injured hand, press it against his cheek, kiss her palm. But she pulled it away. "*Denki*, Stephen." She couldn't seem to meet his eyes, and two flags of color flew on her cheekbones.

What did that mean?

Could she have been as affected as he was by such a simple touch of hands? Was this going to be even more difficult than he'd imagined? But no, she'd already hustled away to the refrigerator, leaning in and rattling the vegetable bins to see what was in there. By the time she'd emerged with a handful of carrots, her color had returned to normal.

Their borrowed dinner was delicious—mashed potatoes mixed with sour cream and dried chives, carrot coins in butter, and the casserole. Beet pickles and the regular cucumber kind rounded out the meal.

"I don't want to get too fancy or wasteful," Susanna admitted, passing him a second helping of carrots. "We don't know how long we'll be stuck here eating Sara and Josh out of house and home."

"At least we won't run out of eggs," he said. "I'll have to break a trail to the barn tomorrow morning anyway, to check on the horses, so I can collect them after."

"Let's leave tomorrow's trials for tomorrow. For all we know, you could be digging a tunnel out there."

Anything was possible in a freak storm like this. But for now, he was in a warm kitchen eating dinner with the one person on earth he never thought he'd see again. Whatever *der Herr* was up to would no doubt be revealed in His own time. In the meanwhile, Stephen was going to count these hours with her as an awkward, uncomfortable sort of blessing.

"Can I ask you something?" she said, cleaning up the last of the casserole on her plate with her fork.

Lulled by a contentment that sparkled along the edges with his awareness of every movement she made, he said, "Sure."

"Where did you go when you left us—I mean, the Four Winds Ranch?"

His fingers lost their dexterity and he dropped his fork with a clatter. Beet pickle juice spattered his shirt front like drops of blood. "What?" He dipped his paper-towel napkin in his water glass and dabbed at it.

"I'm sitting three feet away from you. You heard me."

"You startled me, that's all."

"It wasn't meant to be a startling question. I've been waiting for you to tell me."

"And you thought now was the time?" He gave up on his shirt and tossed the crumpled paper towel beside his plate. "There are some things I don't want to talk about, Susanna."

"Why not?"

A two-word question that would probably take two hours to answer. "Because it's not my place."

"Not your place to tell me the name of a place?"

"That's right."

"*Ich verstehe nicht.*"

Of course she didn't understand. And he wasn't about to enlighten her. In fact, maybe he'd just find something to do that would take him outside for a while.

"*Denki* for dinner. I'm going to shovel off the back steps. Less to do in the morning."

In the mudroom he shrugged on his coat, put on his boots and hat, and let himself out into the whispering snow.

At which point he realized the shovels had been put away in the barn months ago. There certainly wasn't one conveniently leaning on the wall, as there might be in March, nor had there been one in the generator shed when he'd checked the gas. With a sigh, he peered through the whirling maelstrom in the direction of the barn. What he needed first was a rope that he could tie to the railing. If he didn't make it to the barn, at least he could guide himself back to the house. But rope was likely neatly coiled up in the barn, too. Outside of tying the Miller bedsheets together to make one, the only thing he could do was kick and scrape the snow aside with his feet.

The racket he made formed bass notes to the clink of plates and pots in the sink inside. Both of them making noise instead of talking. Confessing. Forgiving.

But that was all right. He had to keep the wall high between them. Because if she succeeded in bringing down even one stone, the whole edifice he'd been constructing from the moment he'd seen her again would collapse.

And he wasn't certain he'd be able to walk away this time.

When his efforts to clear the snow away from the bottom of the steps became a frustration, the heavy drifts collapsing into any area he cleared, he gave up. Knocking the snow off boots and pants, he cleaned himself up as best he could before he let himself back into the mudroom. As he took off his boots and coat, he saw that the kitchen was spotless and orderly, and the scent of coffee in the air told him she'd already prepared the pot sitting on the stove for the morning.

He found her curled in her chair, a book in her lap, reading by the light of the pole lamp.

"Good book?"

She glanced at the cover as if to remind herself of its title. "*Anne's House of Dreams*. Sara must have borrowed it from Aendi Naomi."

"Anne, like *Anne of Green Gables*?"

"*Ja*, they have all Lucy Maud Montgomery's books up at the Circle M. Some are from when Naomi's mother was a girl. It's different to read them now that I know Emily and her family from Prince Edward Island. Cale told us all kinds of stories about their home when they were here at Christmas."

Vaguely, he remembered his sisters reading the first book aloud to each other, going faster on the exciting parts. Someone had a slate broken over his head, he recalled. And somebody else had a boat capsize under them and they had to climb the piling of a bridge.

Then what she'd said sank in. "Cale? Is that your friend's father?"

With a smile, she shook her head. "Brother. Caleb. He's quite the storyteller. He also had quite the crush on Ruby Wengerd."

"The bishop's daughter who's engaged to your cousin?"

"The very one. I guess if nothing else, Cale can be happy he had a hand in making Zachary see the light."

Something in her face told him maybe her memories of this Cale might be a little sweeter than she was letting on. "So when you read about this place, you think about your friends there?"

She lifted one shoulder in a shrug. "I suppose so. I have a standing invitation to visit. I'd like to see it—the scenes she describes." She tapped the book, indicating *she* meant the author. "There are three church districts there—the Kuepfers live in the one on the southwest end."

Stephen didn't know one end of the place from the other. That wasn't the point. "A standing invitation? Nice. From Cale?"

She rolled her eyes and picked up the book. "From his parents, of course."

"But he gave them the idea."

"I'm pretty sure the idea came from Emily. We became *gut* friends, and we're penpals now." Then she frowned at him. "What difference does it make who invited me? The point is, I like them and I'd like to see the place where they live. The place I've been reading about. That no one is afraid to talk about." She dropped her gaze to the pages of the book.

Ouch. Nice, Susannah. Plant the sting right there in the tail.

"I'm not afraid. I made a promise, that's all."

Still looking at the page, she said, "A promise not to say the name of a place. My goodness, that sounds serious."

"There was more to it than that. But *where* would betray a confidence just as much as *why* or *who*."

"A confidence that's a secret?"

"Confidences usually are, *nix*?"

"I suppose so, if you need to hide something."

He should just stop talking.

"Why didn't you say good-bye to us?" Her tone was casual, absorbed. But he was pretty certain she hadn't read a word.

"I had to leave in a hurry. I arranged a trailer for Clancy and a seat up front in the truck for me, and the outfit picked us up the next day."

"I knew Clancy went with you," she said to the book. "I figured either you'd ridden him to the station and put him on a freight train, or else you'd sold him to someone off the ranch."

"I would never sell Clancy," he said, a little offended. "Or if I did, I'd sell him back to your mother. No one else."

"I'm glad to hear it." She looked up and smiled. "When the Eicher turnout went past the other day, I recognized him right away. He looks good. The valley grass must agree with him."

"The Bar K certainly does. I work best on a ranch that cares for their animals as much as for their people. Josiah is fair, and a *gut* husbandman."

"I hope they won't be missing you too much."

He nodded. "It is a worry. I mean, I'm sure they're not worried about me and Clancy, but who knows how many hands got caught out in this. Josiah is going to have to rope in the girls if he needs help to rescue the stock."

"If they're like the Four Winds or the Circle M, needs must. Just don't tell Dave Yoder—he doesn't approve." Her sarcastic tone lightened. "I'm still adjusting to not being a ranch hand myself. But on the *gut* side, I can tell you what the trout are biting in every stream in the valley."

She surprised a laugh out of him. "*Gut* to know. Maybe one day this summer I'll get to go fishing. Now I know who to ask."

"Gideon and Seth will sell you some flies, and happily show

you all their favorite spots. There's a really nice hole on the Circle M, from what they tell me."

How gently she'd turned away the hint that had come out of his mouth without thinking. He tried not to feel rebuffed. It was for the best—they weren't getting back together or anything. But he was going to have to watch himself more carefully.

"So," she mused, "you left without warning believing it was going to be permanent, for a reason that has to be kept secret. That sounds a bit alarming."

"Susanna," he said in a warning tone. "I am not going to talk about this."

"So you said. But you must have been going to a ranch, or you would have left Clancy and his tack at the Four Winds. And it must have been an Amish ranch, or you wouldn't be so close-mouthed about it. Nobody cares what happens on worldly people's places."

This was shooting far too close to the center circle. "Susanna, for heaven's sake."

"So an Amish ranch close enough to trailer a horse to, but not so far away you'd have to put him on the train. Seems like Colorado would fit the bill. And you knew the Schrocks there in Monte Vista from before."

With a burst of annoyance, he jumped off the sofa and glared at her. "Stop it. Just stop."

"Bull's-eye."

"Why won't you leave my business alone?"

"Wasn't me involved in something that can't be talked about," she said mildly. "I'm just making conversation."

"You are not! You're trying to weasel information out of me. It's private, Susanna. Got that?"

"*Ja,* sure."

Ha. Look at Miss Meek and Mild there. She was only gathering her arrows for another try at the target. Though why she bothered was beyond him—*where* and *who* were already out. He just had to do his level best to keep from letting *why* escape, too.

❧ 9 ❧

SUSANNA'S MIND turned like a mill wheel, grinding facts finer and finer, trying to make something palatable out of them. Or if not palatable, then at least something that made sense.

What did she know of the Schrocks in Monte Vista? Next to nothing. All she knew was that Stephen had spent several years on their ranch as a hand after leaving home at sixteen, and they had eight children who would be grown up by now. But what would draw him back there in such an all-fired hurry? It was one thing to hop on the bus with a backpack and go to the aid of a friend. It was quite another to go to the trouble and expense of trailering a horse across two states.

You didn't do that on a whim. A move like that was final.

Which meant that whatever had taken him back to Colorado, it had been important—more than a relationship with her, more than a good job, more than anything. What could be that important to a man?

A death in the family? But that wouldn't mean a permanent visit, unless the person who had passed had willed him the ranch or something. Which clearly wasn't the case, since he'd moved on to the Siksika less than a year later.

A crisis of some kind? Again, crises tended to flare up with intense heat, and then die away once they were dealt with. They weren't permanent, thank heaven.

A desperate call for help? Gazing sightlessly at *Anne's House of Dreams*, she turned that possibility over. Stephen would have to have strong emotions about the person calling. Strong emotions of a lasting kind that would precipitate packing up Clancy and leaving the Ventana Valley for good.

Only one thing fit those criteria.

A woman.

Her stomach rolled over with a sickening lurch.

Who was Susanna, after all, to believe that once he'd loved and lost her, he'd remain unattached forever? Talk about *hochmut*—thinking so highly of herself. *Neh*, of course there had been someone else. He and the Schrock family were old friends. It made perfect sense that he would stay in touch—even once he'd come to work for her family, he'd gone to Monte Vista for Christmas after his own family had come to visit at Thanksgiving. He hadn't said it was to see someone in particular, mind you. Just that he had been invited.

He'd come back, and life had gone on as usual for months, and then suddenly—

How many months?

Stephen had left in early September. Within a day or two of fulfilling his contract for roundup, he'd gone, with barely enough time to make arrangements for Clancy. In fact, he'd left their ranch practically the moment the dust had settled behind the cattle trucks and he'd been given his pay envelope.

Almost nine months.

The sick feeling in the pit of her stomach spread along her

nerves, turning her hands cold, and stiffening her shoulders, as though she'd stepped outside in the snow.

On the sofa, he was gazing at the fire through the glass in the door of the woodstove. What was he thinking? Of that woman? And if he was, why hadn't he stayed with her? Had she had his baby? What had she thought when he'd moved to the Siksika? For that matter, what had her family and the church thought?

Susanna closed the book and set it aside. Suddenly she couldn't bear to read any more about a happy couple newly married and in their first home. She couldn't bear to be in the same room with her own thoughts. Or with him.

What was preventing him from simply telling her, for goodness sake? If a girl had been pregnant as a result of his visit at Christmas, she wouldn't have been able to keep *that* a secret. What was the point of keeping such a secret now that the baby was born? Susanna's frustration and loss and jealousy boiled up inside her, and she was no more capable of keeping the words back than of driving home in this blizzard.

She swung her feet to the floor and stood. "Did you get someone pregnant in Monte Vista?"

Startled, he stared up at her, his mouth falling open in shock. The color drained out of his face. "What—how—what are you talking about?"

"It's a simple question. Did you? Is that why you left the Four Winds so suddenly? Because you heard you were going to be a father?"

Now the blood rushed back into his face and he got to his feet, too—slowly, as though he were trying to control his body as well as his temper. "Is that what you think of me? Really, Susanna?"

"I don't know *what* to think of you. You won't tell me. But it fits. That's the only thing that would have taken you away from me for good—if something happened when you were out there for Christmas, and you had to go and do the right thing almost nine months later."

A laugh cracked out of him. "That's what brought on this insulting line of questions? The fact that I left after roundup and it just happened to be nine months later?"

"You tell me what happened, then."

"I said I wasn't going to talk about it, and I meant it."

"Because you're protecting her?"

"Who?"

"The girl. Maybe one of the Schrock girls, maybe someone else. How should I know?"

"Don't you bring them into it!" He got control of himself, but it took a moment. "It's amazing to me what you think you know when you don't know a blessed thing. Why am I even standing here listening to it?" He glared at her. "I'd rather risk my life out in the snow than stay here one more second."

He stomped through the kitchen, into the mudroom, and shoved his feet into his boots, then grabbed his coat. Fuming, he headed back through the house to the front door.

"Stephen, you can't go out there."

"Don't tell me what to do!" He whirled on her. "Better yet, why don't you make something up? You seem to be so good at it."

"I wouldn't have to," she shrieked, "if you'd only tell me the truth!"

He wrenched open the door and an avalanche of the snow that had been piled up against it came in. A dark figure as big as a snowman fell face first into the living room, and from somewhere in the chaos came the cry of a child.

❦

SUSANNA WAS SO SHOCKED THAT FOR AN ENDLESS, HORRIFIED moment, she thought that the phantom woman they'd been fighting about had actually come and brought him his child.

In the next second, her mind cleared and she realized what she was looking at.

"Shut the door," she said to Stephen. He was so stunned himself that he actually did as she asked. "Help me get this blanket unwound. They're probably frozen half to death."

With gentle hands, he pulled away the snow-covered blanket—no, it was one of those factory-made quilts from a big-box store. It was soaked nearly through, and so was the woman they found inside it, curled around a child who was sobbing weakly against her chest.

"Poor little thing," Susanna murmured to the child, her heart going out in pity. "Did you get a surprise when Mama fell?"

She lifted the child out of the woman's unresisting arms. A boy, barely four years old, with burnished mahogany skin and an explosion of curls soaked flat against his skull.

"Miss?" Stephen said, taking one of the mother's ice-cold hands and chafing it. "Are you all right? Can you hear me?"

"C-cold," came the faint reply.

Stephen looked up. "That coffee on the stove. I'll get it going. I can dry off the *Kind* while you get her into a warm bath. No telling how far she walked, but she might have frost-bite. She's only wearing sandals."

Holy smokes. Susanna knew the signs of frostbite as well as any rancher, but couldn't see the woman's toes through the woven sandals, crusted with snow as they were.

While Stephen got the child out of his wet clothes and

carried him into the kitchen, Susanna coaxed the woman out of her useless shoes. A quick glance told her that frostbite wasn't one of their worries. Hypothermia still might be.

"Come on," she urged softly. "Let's get you into a nice warm bath."

"So cold. Walked—Matty? Where's Matty?"

"He's in the kitchen with Stephen, the foreman from a local ranch," Susanna said in the soothing voice she used with the twins when they woke frightened in the night. "I bet they're looking for applesauce cake. Come on, now. We need to get you warmed up."

The woman found it difficult to walk, but with Susanna's help she was soon chest-deep in a steaming bath. Tears trickled down her face.

"Your light—it saved our lives," she whispered. "My feet—"

"Can you feel them?"

The water swished as she wiggled her toes. "They're coming back. I think. I'm sorry we made a mess."

"Don't you worry about that. It's only water. I'm Susanna. Stephen and I are taking shelter here, too. He came to bring Joshua a saddle to repair—Joshua's the man who lives here with his wife, Sara, and their baby, Nathan. I came to get some elderberry syrup. And before we knew it, the snow was six inches deep and we couldn't get home."

"Are the people who live here ... all right?"

"Oh, yes. They're in Libby. Nathan had to have his shots. What's your name?"

"Zefra."

"Oh, that's pretty. Like zephyr, a soft wind."

The young woman might have smiled. "That's what my auntie says. Though sometimes she says I'm more like a mistral."

"What's that?"

"The opposite—a harsh hot wind."

Susanna made a face at herself. That pretty much described her about ten minutes ago. She shuddered to think what Zefra and Matty's unexpected arrival might have saved her and Stephen from. When would she learn to rule her tongue?

Zefra straightened and the water sloshed around her. "Okay if I use some shampoo? I think my hands will work now. I've never been so cold in all my life."

"First visit to Montana?" Susanna reached down the shampoo bottle from its caddy and handed it to her.

"Yeah. And probably my last. Can you see if Matty is okay?"

"Of course." Susanna rose from her seat on the side of the tub. "You have a good wash and I'll go find a robe or something for you. And rescue a piece of cake for each of us before the menfolks eat it all."

She left Zefra smiling, which gave her confidence that she might yet be all right.

❦

STEPHEN WAS NO STRANGER TO UPSET CHILDREN, THOUGH HE had to admit this was the first one in his experience who had come in from a blizzard. The house was warm, and the little boy was recovering from his ordeal, so once he had wolfed down a piece of cake, he explored his new surroundings in nothing but a pair of underwear with some kind of cartoon character on the rear.

"Don't touch the stove," Stephen cautioned him when the child stretched out his hands to its warmth. "Hot. It will burn you, and then we'll have to take you outside to put your hands in the snow."

The child's eyes rounded, and he stepped cautiously away, eyeing the stove. No more snow for him, evidently. Then his gaze took in the empty living room. "Mama?"

Susanna emerged from the bathroom. "Hi Matty. She's in here, having a bath. Want to have one, too?"

He ran into the bathroom on his chubby legs, and Susanna barely had time to whip off his underpants before Stephen heard a splash and the murmur of his mother's voice.

Stephen pulled a couple of the kitchen chairs in front of the stove, then the two of them draped the pair's soaked clothing over them to dry. The echoes of their argument rang in Stephen's ears, but somehow, the fight had been knocked out of him. Zefra and Matty had bigger problems than he and Susanna did at the moment.

It was almost as though *der Herr* had declared a time-out and sent mother and son in to prevent words that could never be taken back. Though he doubted the half-frozen young woman would see it that way.

"I'll take the blanket downstairs and send it through the wringer," Susanna said, gathering up the sodden mess. "I hope the clothesline is still up. See if you can find a dressing gown for Zefra."

"And maybe some dry clothes for Matty."

"He's older than Nathan ... but maybe we'll get lucky and Nathan's already got some hand-me-downs for when he's older."

In thirty minutes or so, their unexpected guests were cuddled up in a corner of the sofa, warm and dry and comfortable in Sara's nightie and robe and a threadbare but still serviceable pair of pajamas from the little dresser in Nathan's room.

"I don't know how to thank you for helping us," Zefra said from behind her coffee cup. She had polished off her piece of cake, and she and Matty were sharing some of the Zook cheese toasted under the broiler on thick slices of bread. "Thank goodness for the light."

"We put it in the window for just that reason," Stephen said. "With the power out in the valley, we thought anyone who was stranded might be able to see it."

"You're lucky you weren't run over," Susanna added. "When we tried to leave earlier, a diesel rig nearly hit us. He didn't see us until he was on us."

"How far did you have to walk?" Stephen asked.

"I don't know," Zefra confessed. "A long way. We stayed in the car once I couldn't see to drive, and then when it ran out of gas I knew I had to get Matty to a house before we both froze to death."

"Welcome to spring in Montana," Susanna said wryly. "Though I have a feeling this will be one for the record books. We'll be telling this story when we're old and grey, like Aendi Annie." She explained to Zefra, "Annie King is the oldest person in the church here, and she loves to tell her blizzard story."

"Are you sure Joshua and his family won't mind?" Worry filled Zefra's brown eyes.

Susanna shook her head. "I'm sure. He's my cousin. And anyway, I don't imagine anyone in this whole valley will mind if people come knocking on the door." She smiled. "After all, we could be entertaining angels unawares."

Zefra made a noise in her throat. "It's you guys who are the angels."

"Not us," Stephen said lightly, doing his best not to look at Susanna. She knew as well as he that they had been behaving like the exact opposite moments before Zefra and Matty had fallen through the door. "Where were you headed?"

She shook her head. "A dude ranch somewhere around here. The Rocking Diamond?"

Susanna's eyebrows rose. "They share a property line with the Circle M—that's the ranch where my cousin Joshua was raised. Were you going there for a vacation?"

A smile flickered on Zefra's lips. "Not likely. No, I'm supposed to start work there on the first of June. Tomorrow." Her gaze moved to the darkening window, where the pole lamp still burned. "Guess I'll be late for work. My phone died a while ago, or I'd call."

"I don't think they'll be in any position to complain," Susanna said. "What will you be doing?"

"My title is domestic manager, but I understand from my interviews that the job involves more than that. Not only running the household, managing meals, and ordering supplies, but helping Mrs Madison run the guest side of the business, too."

"My goodness," Susanna said. "But Marina Valdez was to have left that job in March, I thought. I wonder if she stayed until the job was filled. Or has Taylor Madison been managing her house herself all this time?"

Stephen bit back a smile. Clearly Susanna had met this *Englisch* person, and didn't think much of her.

"My mother interviewed for the job, too," Susanna explained, maybe to make up for her tone. "But it involves a lot of technology. And we're Amish. So..."

"I wondered if you were. That would make it pretty difficult," Zefra acknowledged. "In any case, Marina did stay on. I was lucky to get the job—it comes with a small house for Matty and me, and Mrs Madison doesn't mind Matty being with me while I work until he's ready to go to kindergarten."

"There's a school practically across the road," Susanna said. "An Amish school. Even a five-year-old could walk there easily."

While she and Zefra talked about the differences between an Amish and an *Englisch* school—and the similarities— Stephen watched her without making it obvious he was watching her. How could this warm, concerned woman be the virago who had shrieked at him less than an hour ago?

Shows you what you're capable of driving a woman to. Why don't you just tell her and put an end to it?

It's not my story to tell.

You know it is. You were smack in the middle of it, and it's only by the grace of Gott you didn't ruin your life as well as Lena's.

I promised.

And you've stood by it. But do you think Lena would want you to sacrifice your future on the altar of her past?

The side that always wanted to do the right thing had no answer to that. Because Stephen had made that decision long ago, when it had seemed vitally necessary. When there seemed to be no other choice.

But what if things were different now? What if *der Herr* had brought him to this valley to give him a choice? Whose promises would count the most then?

EXHAUSTED and sleepy from the hot food and the warm stove, Zefra was ready for bed a short time later. She apologized, but Susanna shook her head as she puttered around the room, making sure the young woman had a glass of water and a lamp. "You've been through an ordeal, and sleep will be the best thing for you. We Amish don't stay up very late. People who are courting might, but..." Her voice trailed away.

No courting was going on here, for sure and certain.

"Courting." Zefra smiled. "That's what they do in the books I like. Regency romances. *Bridgerton.*" When Susanna must have looked blank, she added, "Books set in Jane Austen's time."

"Ah," Susanna said. "I like Jane Austen. I have all her books at home."

"So do I." Zefra tucked the sleeping Matty under the quilt on the guest bed. "This is beautiful. Did your cousin's wife make it?"

The quilt had turned up rather mysteriously, like many of the things that had been in the formerly abandoned house, once Sara had returned from Seattle. "I don't think so. This was Sara's family home. She lost her whole family in a buggy accident and ran away. She came back almost two years ago, and when the church knew she planned to stay, people began to bring back the family's things." She ran a hand over the stitching. "I think her mother probably made this."

Zefra's eyes were sad. "Poor Sara. How awful."

"I'm glad she has something her mother made," Susanna said slowly. "A lot of love went into this. It's a Delectable Mountains pattern."

"Because of the mountains here?"

Susanna lifted a shoulder. "Could be. If you want to see another beautiful one, my cousin Malena made the one in Sara and Joshua's room. It was a wedding gift."

Zefra yawned so widely her jaw cracked. "Maybe tomorrow."

"Of course." She turned to leave them to their rest. "If you or Matty need anything in the night, I'll be right next door."

"Where's Stephen going to sleep?"

She had that look in her eye, the one that wondered if he was more to Susanna than merely a friend. Best to nip that thought in the bud. "Stephen and I dated awhile back, but we broke up," she said in a low voice. "There are four guest rooms —he'll have his choice."

"Why did you break up?" Zefra asked in the same confidential tone. "I was married, but after Matty was born, he decided he was too young for the whole wife and family thing, so he left."

"Too *young?*" How could a man abandon his family for such a reason? And Zefra couldn't be much older that she was. "Was there a big age difference between you?"

She shook her head. "Young in his own mind, I guess, not body. We were the same age."

"Oh." She'd heard of Amish marriages breaking up, maybe in cases of physical abuse or criminal behavior, but never because someone thought he was too young to be seen as a family man. "I'm sorry."

"Don't be. Now I'm free to go where my skills take me. Believe me, from what I've seen so far, it's better that Matty grows up here rather than Chicago. Despite the blizzards."

Susanna smiled in agreement and slipped out of the room, leaving the door ajar so the heat would still come in. Halfway down the hall she realized she hadn't answered Zefra's question. Well, with any luck, the young woman was so tired she'd forget she asked it.

Stephen was adding wood to the stove when she returned to the sitting room and the comfortable embrace of the armchair. He glanced up. "Everyone tucked in?"

"*Ja*. They're exhausted. Sleep will be *gut* for both of them."

"Sleep and safety," Stephen agreed. "We'll figure out everything else tomorrow."

"*Sufficient unto the day is the evil thereof,*" she quoted. "Though I hope there isn't very much evil. I hope most people caught out on the highway were able to get to safety."

"I'm glad Zefra and Matty were. The mother-bear courage of his *mamm* probably saved that little boy's life." With a minute or two before he could close the stove's damper, he walked over to the pole lamp, picked up the five-gallon propane can under it with both hands, and gave it a shake. "It's got about a third left. We can either leave it burning and have none in the morning, or turn it off and save it."

Susanna nibbled her lip. "We might save the propane, but lose a person needing shelter. I don't think I could live with that. Besides, there's always the one in the kitchen for morning."

"You're right." He adjusted the lamp so it didn't burn so brightly, then returned to the stove. He'd put in a keeper, she saw. A chunk big enough to burn all night. He closed the damper, slid the air intake a little more closed, and nodded over his shoulder at the pole lamp. "That should give us eight hours or so, and even on low, the light will be visible for a good way, considering all the other lights are out."

Us. We. How strange that even after their blowup earlier, they had fallen into the plural without even thinking about it. Agreed on what to do sensibly and quietly. As if it would never occur to either of them to shout.

Maybe he was as sorry about losing his temper as she was.

He straightened, and stretched his back. "Well, I guess I'll turn in."

She had slept away from home a few times, but even then, the families she'd stayed with had said their prayers together before bed. Now, with goodness knew what disasters going on outside these walls, an appeal to *der Herr* seemed like more of a necessity than ever.

"Will you say prayers with me before you go?" He gazed at her, and she could practically hear herself in his memory, screeching. She lowered her gaze. "I'm sorry I shouted at you. Please forgive me."

After a moment, he settled on the sofa and clasped his hands between his knees. "I'm sorry I raised my voice to you, too. I don't think there can be too many prayers going up to *Gott*'s ears tonight."

A silence fell, punctuated by the pop of sap in the stove, and she closed her eyes in silent appeal.

Father God, I pray Thou wouldst be with the people caught in this storm. Please guide them to safety and shelter, and protect them through this night. Be with us, Father, with Stephen and me and Zefra and Matty, and the horses and chickens out in the barn. May Thy hand close around us to keep us safe—Josh and Sara and Nathan in Libby, and my family at the Inn, and my family at the Circle M. May Thy love and care be a warm comfort to them—especially Mamm, who worries. And Father, I don't know why you brought Stephen and me together in this house under these circumstances, but I pray Thou wouldst help me to control my tongue, and have a spirit more like Jesus. Stephen may not love me anymore, but I would like it if he were my friend. In Thy Son's holy name I pray, amen.

When Stephen lifted his head a minute later, his eyes met hers and he smiled. She felt as though a calming hand had been laid upon her, enough that she was able to smile back and mean it.

She rose. *"Guder nacht."*

"Sleep well, Susanna."

In the bathroom, she washed her face, then rubbed a little toothpaste on her teeth in lieu of a toothbrush.

It had been a long time since she had heard him say her name like that.

The way he used to at the end of an evening at the Four Winds, when he had to return to the bunkhouse. As though he was sorry they had to say good night at all.

THE OLD PLANK FLOOR IN THE HALLWAY CREAKED, AND Stephen came out of a surprisingly deep sleep the way he always woke—fully alert. A ranch foreman couldn't spend ten minutes waking up slowly and clearing his head—or depending on coffee to do it—not when it meant a calf might die, or someone might not survive an accident.

He listened, then heard the alto murmur of Zefra's voice as she helped Matty in the bathroom. That guy back in Chicago, the one who thought a family made him old, was a fool to walk away from a woman like her. Stephen smiled to himself. Susanna probably hadn't realized earlier that he could hear their conversation. And could also hear the question that she hadn't answered.

Why did you break up?

A question most people could probably answer. But Susanna hadn't. Couldn't. Because while she might be able to say, "He left," he hadn't told her the reason why.

He was still of two minds about it. When they'd said their prayers, he'd even begged the Lord to give him wisdom, to show him the path he should take. Because if he broke his promise to Lena and her family, then Susanna would understand why he'd gone. But the trouble was, before he'd ridden away, there had been an unspoken promise between himself and Susanna. One that he'd broken by leaving with no intention of coming back.

He supposed that in some sad way, it was fitting that a broken promise should go with his own broken heart.

That was the hardest part of this whole untenable situation he was in. How had it been possible to break a good woman's heart because of his desire to do the right thing? He had been caught on the horns of the worst dilemma a man could imagine: No matter which choice he made, a woman would be hurt. In the end, the woman under *die Meinding* had won, because she had no one, and Susanna had a large, loving family who would see her through the worst of his desertion.

And what did that net you in the end? You lost both of them, thus proving you are the biggest Narre that ever lived.

Who wouldn't know the right thing to do if it swatted him on the nose.

He was just drifting off when the floor creaked again. Out of habit, he picked up his watch and pressed the button that illuminated the face.

Two twenty.

A moment later, the water ran in the kitchen, and he heard a glass being filled. If Susanna was up, he should probably check whether the stove needed another piece of wood. He'd barely got his pants and shirt on when he heard the stove door open. Tucking in his shirt, he walked down the hall and out into the living room.

"Let me do that," he whispered.

She stepped out of the way while he chose a likely chunk, and went back into the kitchen to fill the glass a second time. She brought it to him and took two steps toward the hallway that led back to the bedrooms.

"*Denki.* Don't go just yet."

She looked a little surprised, but she came back, and would have settled into the armchair if he hadn't seated himself and patted the sofa cushion next to him.

Surprise seemed to root her to the spot.

"Sound carries," he whispered. "And I have something to say."

A deer could not have edged around a meadow to avoid a hunter more carefully than Susanna edged around the coffee table and settled gingerly on the sofa. He banked the woodstove and returned to his seat, then knocked back half the water in the glass to give himself a moment to organize his thoughts.

Then, he turned to face her. "Earlier, I prayed that *der Herr* would show me His will about the burden I've been carrying for nearly a year. You see, when I left Monte Vista a few weeks ago—" He lifted a hand as she opened her mouth to speak, and she closed it again. "*Ja*, you guessed right—that's where I've been. But when I left to come here, I had no idea your family had moved here, too. Last I heard, you were still on the Four Winds, and something inside me hoped that someone else had snapped you up. That you were happily married. Because then, I wouldn't feel so guilty for what I had done."

"Stephen—"

"Please—" His throat closed and he tried again. "I won't be able to get this out if I don't say it all at once."

She nodded, and reached for the water glass. She took a gulp, as though her mouth had gone as dry as his.

"You can imagine how I felt when I learned that not only had *Gott* opened up the way to a *gut* job here, He had gone further than that. Here you were, in the same valley—the same church district, even—and you were still *eenzich*."

Still single. Heaven help him.

Color flooded her cheeks, and it was all he could do not to reach for her and take her into his arms. Because once he kissed those trembling lips, he would never have the courage to say what had to be said. To give her all the facts. And then leave the decision up to her.

"Tonight, you asked me if I left the Four Winds because I heard I was going to be a father." When she bit her lips, he went on, "I got angry, not because I thought you were making it up, but because you'd come far too close to the truth."

Her cornflower-blue eyes widened, and he was certain she stopped breathing for a moment.

"It wasn't me who put Lena Shrock *im e familye weg*, but it was me who offered to be a father to the child."

The silence was like a still pond in which the ripples of her shock could almost be felt. Her mouth had fallen open but nothing came out. In all the time he'd known her, this was the first time he'd seen Susanna Miller at a loss for words.

"When I visited the Schrocks that Christmas, I heard rumors that Lena was seeing someone who wasn't baptized—who, in fact, was still running around when he was something like twenty-eight. He'd come back to his parents' ranch a couple of times to try to be Amish, and during one of those times, he and Lena had become close. Had decided to marry once he was baptized. Come to find out, by spring one thing had led to another."

"Maybe ... because she thought they would be man and wife," Susanna whispered. "Maybe she committed herself to him, hoping he would commit to the church."

"I don't know," he admitted. "She never said so during the times we talked, but it could have happened that way. We were *gut* friends, and I was happy to be a *Bruder* she could talk to, because for sure and certain she couldn't talk to anyone in her family. She was the only girl left at home, and ... the spirit in that home had changed from when I used to live there. She said it was because of the oldest boy's being killed in a stampede a couple of years before. I don't know. It was just different. Anyhow, I came back to the Four Winds and it was calving time and we were busy. It was a while before she wrote to tell me what had happened after I'd gone back to New Mexico."

"The man she loved was killed?"

He shook his head. "Worse. They were supposed to

THE AMISH COWBOY'S MISTAKE

announce at a big supper for both their families that he would be taking baptism classes so that they could get married in the autumn. But he never turned up."

She sat back on a long breath. "Oh, no."

"She got a postcard from somewhere in the South a month later saying that he was sorry, but he was never coming back and she should forget him."

"And then she found out—"

"*Ja.* She was expecting. Already three months along."

"Ach, the poor girl."

"Her next letter told me that the bishop had put her under *die Meinding,* and her parents had thrown her out of the house."

"But she meant to be this man's wife. She wasn't being a loose woman, *nix?*"

"What she meant didn't hold any water, I guess. She was able to stay with a worldly friend, but it wasn't a permanent arrangement. She didn't know what she was going to do when the baby came."

"What did you do?"

"I wrote back with some suggestions—live with her grand-parents, try to get a job—but when I got her reply at the end of August, she'd come to the end of her rope. First she said she was going to ... do away with herself."

Susanna gasped.

"Then she calmed down and told me she was going to leave the church. Try to find this man, wherever he'd gone, and make a new life for herself."

"It's a better alternative than—than—" She swallowed. "But travel? That late in her pregnancy?"

"I know. She must have been desperate. I was her only

friend, and I felt I'd let her down—left her with no other choice."

"But Stephen, that wasn't your place. It was this man's place. Were you—" Her throat closed. "Did you love her?"

"She and her family have been so good to me. As you know, my family isn't ... close. Not like yours. Or the Keims. The Schrocks became my second family, and Lena and I had become such *gut* friends that ... well, her parents half expected we would marry someday." He glanced up, into those beloved eyes. "But then I got work the next summer on the Four Winds, and I learned the difference between a *gut* friendship ... and real love."

Her eyes filled with tears, and she blinked them back, leaving her lashes spiky and wet. "You loved me?"

Her use of the past tense broke his heart. But he had to leave it there, like an injured creature in the path. Had to finish.

"Lena was like a sister and a best friend wrapped into one. Something inside—a still, small voice—told me that if she actually went through with this plan, that the baby would not survive, and she might not, either. So I called the place where she was living and said I would help her. She was not to do anything until I got there. I waited just long enough to collect my pay, and I put Clancy in the trailer and headed out."

"For good. Or so you thought."

He huffed a laugh at his own expense. "Or so I thought. I found her sleeping on a sofa in her friend's basement, with only a backpack of *Englisch* clothes to her name. She was taking those vitamins pregnant women are supposed to take, but she was as thin as a stick. She'd joke about it. 'I'm like the letter *B* with legs,' she'd say. '*B* for *boppli*.'"

"So what did you do?"

"I asked her to marry me. I told her I would be a father to her child. We would go to the bishop and she would go on her knees before the church and repent. He would lift *die Meinding* and we would be married. I couldn't very well bring a wife to the Four Winds—"

The color drained from her face. "*Denki* for that," she whispered.

"—but I could get work on any ranch in Colorado that provided a married couple's quarters. It was still roundup season, and many places needed help. It was a *gut* plan." He took a long breath that shuddered at the end.

"But ...?"

"But she turned me down flat. Worse, she got angry that I expected her to return to a church that had *treated her like garbage*. Those were her words. She informed me that she had changed her mind about looking for the child's father. She and the girl who lived there had started their own business, she said, cleaning houses in Monte Vista. She didn't need me, or the church, or *Gott*, and she thanked me for coming all that way, but I wasn't to stay and try to convince her. Her mind was made up, and the sooner I got on with my own life, the better."

"Oh, Stephen," she breathed. "She must have been so wounded in her spirit, pushing away her only friend."

He clasped his hands, dangling between his knees, to prevent himself from taking hers.

"You may be right. I stuck around for a few days. I went to the Shrocks' to see if there was any help or mercy there, but they were adamant that the *Bann* would bring her to her senses. Bring her home."

"It doesn't sound like it ever would."

"And it hasn't. I heard from one of her brothers on another ranch. That girl she was staying with? Lena apparently married her brother. An *Englisch* man called Eric Johnson. She'll never see her family again. The *Boppli* will never know its grandparents."

"Was it a girl or a boy?"

He blinked. "I don't know. No one ever said. All I know is that her parents begged me not to tell anyone. They were so ashamed."

Susanna made a face. "Not much point in that. The entire church would have to know."

"I felt it was the least I could do for them. To make that promise so it didn't go farther. We'd been close once, and even if I thought what they'd done was wrong for their daughter, in their minds they were doing *Gott's wille*."

"I'm so sorry. What an awful situation." She was silent a moment. "Now I'm even more sorry that I demanded you tell me. Now that I know, I almost wish I didn't. It's sad, and horrible, and that poor *Boppli* ..."

He sighed, and let some of the stress and tension leave his body with it. "It has been a burden to carry, all through those months of working on any ranch I could, never landing anything permanent. I'm glad it's off my shoulders."

"I won't tell anyone."

"I'm sorry to hand over half of it. But of all people, you had a right to know why I left like a thief in the night. I thought I was doing the right thing. Sent by *Gott* to save someone, like Boaz saved Ruth." He shook his head. "If she'd just called and talked to me, she could have told me to mind my own business *before* I made a decision I couldn't undo."

"But you did undo it," she said. "When *Gott* brought you here, to the Siksika."

But Stephen had thought he was obeying *Gott's wille* when he'd run headlong to Colorado to save a woman who didn't want to be saved. He'd sure give a lot to know what *der Herr* had in mind for him now.

❧ 11 ❧

As she lay in the dark in her borrowed bed, Susanna's mind felt as though a series of dust devils were whirling through it, each labeled with a different name.

Stephen, abandoning his livelihood, riding to another woman's rescue ... and having the door closed in his face.

Lena, who had only to reach out her hand to have everything Susanna ever wanted ... and turning it down.

The Schrocks, grieving the loss of their son ... and in their anxiety not to lose their daughter, pushing her away for good and ever.

No matter the possibilities Susanna could have dreamed up for what had happened after Stephen had left the Four Winds Ranch, the truth had been even more distressing and awful. What a terrible situation—one that could not be resolved now except by the hand of God.

Except for one thing.

Stephen was free.

But at the moment when she thought he would speak—ask her forgiveness for leaving and for intending to marry someone else, tell her he had loved her the whole time—he had not. Instead, he had rubbed his face as though there were tears on his cheeks, got up to check the stove, and wished her *guder nacht*.

She'd sat in the firelight as though paralyzed, waiting for him to come back, but he hadn't. The bed at the end of the hall had creaked, and outside of spending the night on the sofa, she had no option but to go back to bed, too.

To lie there being tormented by dust devils.

It was clear to her now that she had been guilty of *hochmut* repeatedly when it came to Stephen Kurtz. The pride of a woman who believed herself the object of a man's love.

Susanna, you fool. You've done it not once, but twice now—first when you and he were courting on the Four Winds, and second while you were snowed in here, waiting for him to throw himself at your feet.

So much for the grand romance she thought she'd been having. He'd ridden away to throw himself at *Lena Schrock's* feet. And now, when he had confessed it all, in a midnight tryst, the perfect moment to take the next step ... he'd gone to bed.

Wasn't that just like a man.

When was she going to learn that Stephen no longer saw her in that way? Oh, they'd enjoyed their time together on the Four Winds, no doubt about that. And maybe she'd been a little too willing to show her feelings ... but she was made so. She wore her heart on her sleeve, as Mamm often said. She couldn't help it.

Maybe it was time to learn some caution. Some discretion. Because she could only imagine what the *Youngie* here in the Siksika would say if they knew she'd been carrying a torch for Stephen all this time. Loving a man who was oblivious to her, the way poor Sylvia Keim hankered after Tobias. She'd never hear the end of it. She wouldn't give anyone the chance to think of her as *poor Susanna Miller*. And if that wasn't *hochmut*, what was?

She was right back at the beginning, her thoughts going around and around as though they were dancing across the prairie, picking up more and more dirt until something stopped them or they petered out for lack of direction.

It seemed like hours that she lay there, sleepless, watching the rectangle of the window, waiting for morning. But though it was still dark, the window had a peculiar outline. Not black, but not the gray of approaching dawn, either. Surely it must close enough to five that she could get up and start a pot of coffee. She had just swung her bare feet to the rag rug when she sat up straight, listening. Something had changed.

Silence.

The whisper of the snow against the windowpane had stopped.

Oh, please let it have stopped for good. Please let this be over.

She padded barefoot to the window to look out ... and realized why the light was so strange. For she couldn't see the hay field that she knew was on the other side of the fence. Not even a white expanse. Because the east-facing window was completely blocked by snow.

"Oh, my," she whispered, fruitlessly craning to look up, trying to see how high it might go. "Aendi Annie King is going to have competition for her blizzard story now."

The farmhouse did not have two stories, so Aendie Annie still had the advantage there. But if the snow drifted against the house now covered the windows, then it was at least up to the eaves.

Susanna lit the kerosene lamp on the dresser and put her

clothes on quickly, wishing that she had winter socks. She was lucky she'd put on proper shoes yesterday, at least. Not like Zefra in her woven string sandals. They'd have to find her some boots. Susanna did the best she could with her hair, finger combing it, braiding it, and then pinning the whole untidy mess up under her *Kapp*.

Coffee first. And then maybe she could face Stephen with the smile of a friend, and make jokes about taking turns digging a tunnel over to the barn.

Out in the kitchen, she had barely set the match to the burner and put the coffeepot on it when she heard the door of the woodstove open in the living room and then the *scrutch* of the coals being spread to take fresh chunks of wood. The door swung shut and after a moment Stephen joined her in the kitchen.

"The snow is up over the windows," she said in a low voice. It wasn't likely Zefra and Matty were up yet. Not in this weird daylight darkness. "But at least it stopped."

"Hopefully for good, not just for now."

He looked out the four-light window in the mudroom door and whistled. "Susanna. Come look."

On the back porch, which was covered by a sloping roof, a narrow strip of planks was still visible. But the steps were buried in drifts of snow at least as tall as Stephen himself. At the top, between the snow and the porch roof, was enough sky to poke a shovel through.

"We shouldn't touch it," he warned. "If it collapses inward, we won't be able to get the door open."

"Whether it does or it doesn't, there's nowhere to go," she pointed out. "I'm glad you gave the animals extra feed. It's going to take a while to burrow over there."

"Without a shovel," he added, and made a wry face. "I'll be carving paddles out of firewood at this rate."

"Let's go in." She slipped into the warm kitchen gratefully and held the mudroom door for him. "Things will look better after coffee and breakfast."

The clock over the door said it was a little after six on the strangest summer morning she'd ever experienced. It wasn't daylight, exactly, and yet it wasn't dark either. Maybe this was what the books meant when they talked about the land of the midnight sun. Only inside the house.

From the guest room came a thump and the sound of running footsteps. "Matty!" Zefra called, to no avail. The child skidded to a halt on the kitchen linoleum and beamed up at Susanna.

"Juice!" he announced, as though he expected it to appear instantly.

In her borrowed robe, Zefra hurried out. "I'm sorry. He usually gets some orange juice. Matty, we're guests in someone else's house. It's not going to be the same as our apartment."

"Juice." His little face crumpled.

Stephen was already inspecting the contents of the refrigerator as Matty began to sob. "No juice, but it looks like there's milk."

"He's still tired," Zefra said apologetically, accepting a glass. Matty pushed it away, so Zefra drank it herself. Luckily Stephen was prepared with a refill before the chld's indignation found its voice, and this time Matty decided a bird in the hand was better than two in the bush.

Hiding a smile, Susanna got busy mixing up cheese biscuits and scrambling eggs, while Stephen put the salsa on the table and set it for four. Some fried ham slices rounded out their meal, and after filling their mugs, Susanna made a second pot of coffee. Then she and Stephen put the food on the table.

"We say grace before we eat," Susanna said as she seated herself. "A silent grace."

Zefra bent to her son. "Matty, we'll be quiet while Stephen and Susanna say thank you to God for this amazing breakfast."

"Sank you," Matty repeated.

When Susanna raised her head after grace, she found Matty watching her. "I said thank you to God for you, too," she confided to him. "For bringing you safely to us. Now, let's eat."

She passed the biscuits to Zefra and before long, they were laughing and talking as though they were old friends.

"No telling how long it will be before the snow melts," Stephen said, helping himself to another piece of ham. "Looks like we'll have enough food to see us through the day, though."

"I found some hamburger in the freezer section," Susanna added. "Enough to give us two suppers. And there are lots of canned tomatoes in the cellar. I can make spaghetti and meatballs."

"Poor Josh," Stephen said with a grin. "His cupboard will be bare by the time we dig ourselves out."

"I'm amazed there is so much food here when the people aren't even home." Zefra tried not to reach for seconds, but when Susanna pushed the bowl of eggs toward her, she gave in.

"Well, they were expecting to be back tomorrow."

"I'm just grateful," she said. "Some days it's a miracle if I have popcorn and cereal on hand."

"You won't want for anything at the Rocking Diamond," Stephen said. "From what I hear, the staff and hands are treated well, and with a job like yours, you'll be in the big house most of the time anyway."

"If I still have a job by the time we dig ourselves out of here." She gazed over Susanna's shoulder at the window over the sink, and tilted her head. "Is it my imagination, or is there more light now?"

"It's after seven, so the sun will be up over the mountains." Susanna turned to look. "But you're right. It does seem lighter. You don't suppose the snow is melting already, do you? Could we be that lucky?"

"Don't get your hopes up." Stephen scooped up the last of his salsa with a biscuit, then took his plate to the sink.

Matty, who had already cleaned up his eggs and a biscuit slathered in blackberry jam, slid down from the pillow on his chair, picked up his plate, and trotted to the sink with it.

"Thank you," Stephen said solemnly, and took it.

Her eyes wide, Zefra caught Susanna's smile. "May I take your plate?" Silently, the young woman handed it over, then got up to help clear away the food.

While Susanna ran water into the sink, Matty scampered back and forth with one item at a time—a butter knife, the jar of salsa, a spoon. Stephen took each thing with a thank-you, delighting the child.

"Would Matty like to dry?" Susanna asked his mother.

"Oh ... I don't know if that—"

"I'll start with the knives and forks," she said. "If he drops one, it won't matter."

Stephen took a dish towel, and gave the other one to the little boy. He showed him how to dry the cutlery, and because he wasn't tall enough to see into the drawer, picked him up so he could place the pieces in their slots one at a time.

"I can't believe it," Zefra whispered to Susanna when she took her son's dish towel to finish the job. Stephen put Matty's shoes on and they went outside to the back porch to inspect the drifts once more. "I didn't think he knew what dishes were, never mind that forks and knives go in a drawer."

"We teach our children to help as soon as they're able to see over the table," Susanna said. "A little one wants to help like the grownups do, even one as young as four. It helps them feel like part of the family, don't you think?"

"I guess it does," Zefra said, drying the glass mixing bowl. "I just never thought to let him help."

"He may lose interest after a few days, but even so, if that's his job, and he's encouraged to do it, you can give him other things to do, like setting the table and pouring water for everyone."

"I do want to bring him up to look after himself," Zefra said. "How old were you when you learned to cook? You make it look so easy. I have to have a cookbook to boil water."

"I like cooking," Susanna said with a lift of one shoulder. "I started helping my mother when I was pretty young—the only girl with three older brothers. I could make breakfast for everyone by the time I was ten, which was good, because we lived on a ranch and the hands all ate with us."

"Is this a ranch, too?" Zefra put away the last pot.

"No, this is a hay farm. Folks with cattle are grateful for folks with hay farms, especially in February, when every bit of feed matters."

"I guess I have as much to learn as Matty," Zefra said with a sigh. "Maybe tonight we can make the spaghetti and meatballs together? Matty will love them."

Susanna grinned. "We'll make lots of meatballs so you'll have lots of practice."

Zefra grinned back. "And your ex will realize he was crazy to let you go."

It felt as though the world lurched to a halt. "I don't know ..."

"I heard you talking last night. I hope you got some things cleared up."

Susanna had to laugh, a rueful sound without much joy in it. "Some things cleared up ... and some things made more of a mystery than ever."

"He'll come around. You'll see."

Susanna wrung out the dishcloth and walked over to wipe down the cheerful red-and-white checked oilcloth on the table. "You're assuming I want him to."

"I think you do." Zefra's gaze was deep, assessing. "I can see it shining out of your face when you talk to him. He's blind if he can't see it, too."

She felt the hot color suffusing her cheeks. "I hope he doesn't. Because I don't think he cares for me the way he did. If he ever did," she corrected herself.

Zefra was silent a moment. "Girl, if ever a woman could make a man care for her again, it's you. Don't sell yourself short."

Susanna was still recovering from her surprise when the back door opened and Stephen and Matty came in.

"We have company," Stephen announced, and stood to one side.

"*Guder mariye,*" her cousin Adam Miller called cheerfully from out on the porch, bent at the waist. A snowdrift had fallen in, and a big chunk of sky was visible behind him. "Give me a minute to get these snowshoes off. I hope there's still some coffee in that pot—I've been up all night and I could really use it."

AFTER A MOMENT OF STUNNED SURPRISE, Susanna swung into action, getting her cousin a cup of coffee, frying up four eggs, and serving them to him with the remaining biscuits and ham. She had about a hundred questions, and hardly knew which one to ask first.

"Got company, I see," Adam said around a mouthful of ham. He nodded to Zefra. "Adam Miller. I live on the Circle M Ranch, about a mile and a half from here."

"Zefra Harris, and this is my son Matias. Matty."

"Hey Matty," Adam said cheerfully to the wide-eyed child. "Nice to meet you both. Did you manage to get here before the storm hit?"

"No," Stephen said. "After her car ran out of gas, she wrapped Matty in a quilt, and followed the light from the living room window. She's a brave woman."

Zefra flushed at the praise. "I'm supposed to be starting work at the Rocking Diamond today."

"She's replacing Marina," Susanna explained, "and she'll get there when she gets there. Did you really snowshoe here, Adam? It must be almost eight feet deep out there."

"That's the point of snowshoes." He gulped the last of his coffee, and she got up to pour him some more. "Don't worry about the Madisons, Zefra—they've got their hands too full with a bunch of guests and no electricity." He dumped cream into his fresh coffee. "I came across lots. First time I ever went over all those fences without touching them. Your brothers are at the ranch, Suz, going a little nuts hoping you're okay. Which reminds me." He fished a cell phone out of his pocket. "Call your *mamm*."

When Rachel heard her voice, she burst into tears.

"*Mamm—Mamm, ischt okay,*" Susanna said in *Deitsch*, in as soothing a tone as she could. "Adam just got here on snowshoes and brought his phone. I'm at Josh and Sara's with Stephen Kurtz and a young *Englisch* mother and her boy who took refuge with us. We just finished breakfast. We're all right, I promise."

"*Denkes, mei Vater.*" Rachel choked out a prayer. "*Denkes.*"

"Is everyone all right there? What about Tobias? Adam says the boys are at the ranch."

"*Ja*, I've spoken to them both. We haven't heard from Tobias yet, but I'm nearly certain he took refuge on one of the ranches on his route. Oh, Susanna—the sound of your voice is like music to me."

"Don't ask me to sing, Mamm."

Her mother had recovered enough to give the ghost of a laugh.

"And Luke? Have you heard from Will and Zeke?"

"I just talked to Luke. They're going to start digging out. My cousins are worried about the goats."

"Of course they are. Neither rain nor sleet nor eight feet of snow will stop those two from getting to their goats. Mamm, I don't know when I'll be home."

"When *der Herr* allows it, I expect. As long as I know you're safe, I can face anything now. Bless Adam. Give him a big hug from me."

When Susanna disconnected and handed her cousin his phone, she gave him a big hug, as instructed. "That's from Mamm."

He hugged her back. "I'm glad you're okay. It's been an awful night. Especially after the snow got too deep for the EMT van to get through. We've got a soup kitchen going at the fire station, and calls coming in the whole time. Not a thing we could do after about two a.m. except tell people to turn off their engines and bundle up together."

"Surely the plows will be out soon?" Stephen asked.

"They're already out," Adam said. "All two of them. They started on the county highway about five, when the snow stopped. Risk of loss of life takes priority over the people in town safe inside their houses. Nobody is going to work today, anyhow. They're calling it a hundred-year storm." He glanced at Zefra, but she didn't look reassured.

Susanna couldn't blame her. From what Mamm had said about Taylor Madison, even nearly dying in a hundred-year storm was no excuse for being late to work at *her* ranch.

"Adam, do you want to rest here?" she asked. "If you've been up all night, even an hour would help."

"If I lie down for an hour, it'll be twelve," Adam told her, shaking his head. "I'm going to help you guys dig out, and then I'll go home and sleep."

"Dig out with what?" she asked, half serious. "The frying pan and the scrap bucket? The shovels are in the barn."

"The pan and bucket will do for a start." He grinned. "I can't get out the way I came in, that's for sure and certain."

"He slid through that hole on his back," Stephen explained. "Like a cow in a chute, only vertical."

"I've got to move, or I'll pass out where I sit." Adam pushed back his chair. "Thanks for breakfast. Best ever."

He got them organized with anything they could find—the black speckled canner, a trash can, the scrap bucket. Then they formed a line, with Stephen and Adam taking turns scooping out snow and tamping it into rough steps leading up to the surface.

"There's a pretty good crust on top because it was so cold last night," he told them. "If we can get up to it, we can slide across the yard to the barn, at least. We won't get farther than that."

"We won't need to," Susanna panted. "Like you said, no one is going anywhere today."

"Except Adam," Zefra said, heaving snow out of the way with the canner. Matty, in a pair of borrowed boots far too large for him, was making snowballs out of it.

It took half an hour to create a sloping set of rough steps up to the surface, letting in a welcome shaft of daylight.

"Am I hallucinating, or is it warmer?" Stephen wondered aloud. "We'd better hurry. If the crust softens, we'll never get across, never mind back again."

But when he heaved himself out and gingerly tried to walk on the crust, it collapsed under him. Luckily Adam was close enough to grab him and haul him back to safety.

"Okay, next plan?" Stephen was clearly shaken. Being buried in snow over your head was no laughing matter.

"Rugs," Susanna said suddenly. "I've seen pictures of penguins sliding on their stomachs. What if you used rugs to spread the weight and slide like that?" She dashed inside and returned a minute later with two braided rugs from the bedrooms. "Let's hope this works."

Stephen climbed up the makeshift steps once more, laid the rug on the snow, and pushed off on his stomach as though he were on a toboggan. One moment Susanna could see his feet, and they next they were gone. A whoop was carried back to them on the cold air.

"Good enough for me." Adam tossed a grin over his shoulder and climbed up, throwing down the rug and pushing off.

"I have to see this." Susanna took one cautious, slippery step at a time until her head rose into the light above the trampled snow. The sun gleamed off the deep, unmarked expanse, where only lumps indicated there might be a tree or even a shed underneath. All the fences were two and three feet down.

"It's so white it hurts my eyes," she said over her shoulder to Zefra. "But the men have reached the barn on their flying carpets."

"I wish Matty could make a snowman," Zefra said, regret in her tone. "No, baby. It's not safe to touch that stuff near the stairs—it could fall in on you. I like your pile of snowballs, though. You did good. Come on, let's go inside now, where it's warm, and see if our clothes are dry."

Susanna stayed at the top of the snow stairs, keeping vigil long enough to hear rather than see the big barn door slide open with a rumble. Then she climbed down, digging her fingers into the packed snow to keep herself from losing her footing, and slipped into the warm house.

"They made it to the barn and got inside," she reported,

holding out her frozen fingers to the woodstove's heat. "I think the air might have warmed a couple of degrees."

"Let's hope the crust holds long enough for them to get back. Hey, my jeans are almost dry. And Matty's shirt and pants are—they're just cotton. I didn't think to bring his snowsuit in May. Lesson learned."

"Did you have suitcases in the car?"

"Yeah. But I doubt anyone is going to come along and steal them."

"Not likely they can even see it. I sure hope the snow melts enough today that the volunteer fire crew can get people out to safety."

"Not everyone can be as lucky as me," Zefra said sadly, gazing out the window more metaphorically than anything, since it was as blocked up with snow as the rest.

"Not everyone was as *brave* as you, seeing the light and heading for it," Susanna said, giving her shoulder a squeeze. "I'm really glad you did. And after all this is over, think of the story you'll have to tell."

Zefra laughed. "The first person I'm going to tell it to is Taylor Madison. If she doesn't believe me, my career as a story-teller—and a domestic manager—is over."

"The Bible says the testimony of two men is true—and you have three witnesses to back you up. So there, Taylor Madison. Put that in your pipe and smoke it."

With a slightly guilty laugh at her employer's expense, Zefra dressed Matty in his own clothes, socks, and his little running shoes. Then, while Susanna finished up the dishes, Zefra found children's books in Nathan's room. Susanna smiled when she recognized the first story. Zefra was a *gut* reader, making different voices for Mrs Mallard and the policemen helping her to get her ducklings to the park.

Then she leaned in a bit to look more closely at the window. It was to be expected that the warm glass would melt the snow around it. But ... was the gap at the top of the drift against the house looking mushy? Could it really be melting so soon?

Ach, lieber Gott, let it be so!

A very long forty-five minutes later, a series of thumps on the back porch told her that the men were back from the barn. But when Stephen came in, his pants brushed off, and toed off his boots by the mudroom door, he was alone.

"Adam's gone home," he said to Susanna's inquiring look, closing the door behind him and coming into the kitchen. "Temperature's rising. It's above freezing now, and he figured the crust would be too soft for snowshoes if he didn't hurry. I brought a shovel—and the eggs."

From the depths of his jacket he produced a burlap feed sack with a dozen eggs in the bottom.

But Suzanna's attention was still snagged on *above freezing.* She put the eggs in the egg keeper in the refrigerator. "Is there any chance at all of getting home today?"

"I suppose we'll have to wait on the answer to that," he replied. He spotted the package of hamburger she'd set on the counter to thaw. "But I'd be sorry to miss the spaghetti and meatballs."

She rolled her eyes. "Come to the Inn some night and I'll make them for you."

Both of them seemed to realize at the same moment what she'd said.

"*Ja?*" he said, making no move to go into the sitting room to warm up his reddened hands. "I'd like that."

Susanna's face grew so hot he could have warmed his hands

on her cheeks. No, she couldn't think like that. It only made her blush harder.

She had to say something.

"I think Mamm would like to show our family's gratitude for everything you've done here, getting in wood, looking after the animals, helping with—with everything."

"You're the one who's been cooking and cleaning up and taking care of us."

"I agree," came Zefra's voice from the sitting room. That girl had ears like a cat. "If it weren't for both of you, Matty and I would probably be frozen to death. If I had my own house, I'd invite you both over, and Susanna could show me how to make a thank-you dinner."

Laughter broke the tension.

"Tell you what," Susanna said. "If by three o'clock the snow is still too deep for us to walk out and find your car, then we'll have to stay another night. And I'll keep my promise about the meatballs."

"We can call it a thanksgiving dinner," Stephen said. "I don't know about you three, but I have a lot to be thankful for this morning."

His gaze caught hers, and Susanna's breath nearly stopped. Words flew out of her head like startled blackbirds, and all she could do was fall into those green eyes. Once, they'd held all the promise of the future she'd thought was inevitable.

But he had made a choice. Put someone else first.

No one liked to be second choice. The consolation prize. If Stephen Kurtz thought he was going to warm up cold soup with her now that he was free of his promise to Lena Schrock, well ... he had another think coming.

🌿 13 🌿

STEPHEN SAW the moment when the vulnerability and the longing left Susanna's eyes, and resolve came down like a blind over a window. For just one moment, when she'd invited him to the Inn for dinner as though it were the most natural thing in the world, his heart had leaped with hope and he'd been bold enough to tell her how he felt.

That blush had told him she might feel the same way. And then ... whatever her feelings had been, she had roped them in with all the skill she might have used to stop a runaway calf.

Something still stood in their way, and he was going to find out what it was.

But it wasn't likely she'd allow another firelight talk in the middle of the night. *Neh*, he was going to have to do something else—something that would break down the barrier she'd erected and let him in to be what he'd dreamed of.

A man worthy of her love.

Could she still love him? After what he'd done?

As the day wore on, and she treated him with the same smiling friendship she showed Zefra and Matty, he began to doubt himself. He'd been a fool, yes, galloping off to Colorado to be a knight in shining armor, and getting pushed into a metaphorical moat for his trouble. Could Susanna forgive a fool?

Did she want to be married to a fool?

In those dark months after Lena's rejection, before he'd finally left Colorado for the job in the Siksika, he'd convinced himself Susanna would have married someone else, so there was no point in returning to the Four Winds Ranch. He'd often thought of that mythical man he'd made up for her—someone strong in the Lord, loving and sensible, and a *gut* provider. Not a lonely, rejected idiot who didn't know what to do with himself other than work.

At least he had that. A foreman could provide pretty well —*gut* wages, in many cases a house or separate quarters, stability. And he had made a lifetime commitment to the Lord, as had she, that wonderful Communion Sunday when together, they'd covered their faces before the *Gmay* and made their promises to God.

But a loving and sensible man? What did she see when she looked at him? The respected foreman, or the boy who had dumped her flat and gone chasing off to save a woman who didn't want to be saved? That had been neither loving nor sensible. While he had gone with the best and kindest of intentions, it had been a complete mistake. He had fallen victim to his own pride, his own confidence that he knew the answers to all Lena's problems—namely, himself. All wrapped up with a big bow.

Pride goeth before destruction, the Psalmist had so wisely said, *and a haughty spirit before a fall*. Stephen sighed at himself, even as he levered another chunk of wood into the woodstove. He'd worked destruction on a pure and blossoming love, and he wasn't certain that he could win Susanna's heart a second time. Or if he should even try. Surely she deserved someone who made better use of his brain and heart than Stephen ever had.

Anyone would be better.

Except maybe Calvin Yoder. A plague of locusts would be better than him.

Stephen walked back into the guest room he'd been using. There was a Bible in the bookcase, so he pulled it out and sat on the foot of the bed to look up what else the Psalmist had to say on the subject. Instead, the pages fell open at Isaiah 55, and his gaze landed on the words God had spoken to the prophet.

For as the heavens are higher than the earth, so are my ways higher than your ways, and my thoughts than your thoughts. For as the rain cometh down, and the snow from heaven, and returneth not thither, but watereth the earth, and maketh it bring forth and bud, that it may give seed to the sower, and bread to the eater: So shall my word be that goeth forth out of my mouth: it shall not return unto me void, but it shall accomplish that which I please, and it shall prosper in the thing whereto I sent it.

So are my ways higher than your ways.

Sitting on a bed belonging to a couple he didn't yet know, but who had provided him shelter all the same, Stephen found himself humbled by the vastness of the ways of the Lord. Moving pieces, changing lives. Putting His mighty hand in the way of Stephen's headlong flight and saying *no*. Releasing him to a different path—one that would bring him straight back to Susanna.

It shall accomplish that which I please.

Hadn't both he and Susanna been made aware that their separate journeys to the Siksika Valley were more than simply coincidence? Granted, her family was here. Rachel Miller had grown up here. But how did that explain Stephen's getting the job at the Bar K ranch? The odds were astronomical that Josiah Keim would need a foreman at the same time that Stephen needed a job. That Susanna's family would move here within months of Stephen's doing the same. That the two of them would be brought together in the same church district—and yesterday, to the same house.

It was unmistakable.

It shall prosper in the thing whereto I sent it.

How dared he declare that anyone else would be better to fill the place where God had put him? There was humility —*demut*—and there was cowardice. Because touching Susanna's heart was not going to be so easy the second time. Then again, wasn't any task that *der Herr* set for a person made easier simply because all the power of Heaven lay behind it?

The Lord had brought Stephen here to work out His will. And in His goodness and love, He had set Stephen a course that would be nothing but joy to run.

Stephen's heart swelled with such gratitude that his throat ached with it. He slid to his knees and buried his face in his hands, his whole soul a song of thanks. For the mercy he had been shown despite his own foolishness. For the certain knowledge that this—*this*—was finally the right thing, the right path to earthly and heavenly happiness.

In his communion with heaven, he was unconscious of his own body, or of the hard plank floor under his knees. And he did not realize he had left the door cracked open.

SUSANNA HESITATED OUTSIDE IN THE HALLWAY. SHE HAD meant to go in to tell Stephen that he could stop making those little remarks, those little hints that made her blush. The fact that such things had been so precious to her when their courtship was budding and new only made it more necessary that she not hear them now.

But here she stood, frozen, to see him kneeling beside the bed with his back to her, clearly deep in prayer.

And her heart cracked.

She couldn't remember seeing him in prayer when he lived on the Four Winds. Mind you, his quarters were in the bunkhouse, and she had never gone up there with him, because that wouldn't be fitting. Family prayer in the evening was different, because everyone bowed their heads silently. This, now, was strictly between him and *Gott*.

Stop spying on him, Susanna.

Quietly, she closed the bedroom door, turning the handle and releasing it once it was shut, so the latch made no noise. She told herself it was so that little Matty wouldln't run in and interrupt him. But deep down, it was because the sight had affected her so deeply.

She took refuge in the room she was using, closing her door, too. What was it about a praying man that did this to her? She sat on the edge of the bed, hardly seeing the planks bare of the rag rug that was now drying in the kitchen. She and Stephen had been baptized together, sharing the most important ceremony of their lives. Only a wedding came next in importance. She'd fully believed that she would share that sacrament with him, too.

Well, she hadn't. And it wasn't likely she ever would. Because how could she trust that he wouldn't pull up stakes and leave her again, the next time he thought someone needed him? Would he even spare a thought for Susanna's own need?

And yet ... somehow he had become a praying man.

Dat had been like that. She'd seen him more than once, when he was alive, riding fence on Clancy. He'd pull up the big black cutting horse, loosen the reins to make grazing easier, and bow his head. She'd been a little girl when she'd asked him once what he was doing. "Thanking the Lord for little gifts," he'd said, touching her cheek. "Like the lupines growing next to the fence. The scrub jays coming back. And you."

All Plain women wore a head covering so that at any moment of the day, they could approach *der Herr* in prayer, whether they were feeding sheets into the mangle or canning tomatoes or simply walking in the grass, breathing in the scent of growing things. But how many times had Susanna actually done that? Given thanks to *Gott* for little gifts. Lupines. The wild roses that gave their inn its name. Sunny the chicken, who had made her home with them whether they were ready for poultry or not.

And what about the blessing of Stephen's being here in the storm with her and Zefra? Because there was no getting around the fact that Susanna felt completely safe with him in the house. No matter what he'd done in the past, no matter how angry or grieved she'd felt, his presence had always made her feel this way.

Ach, she was mixed up and *verhuddelt* for sure and certain.

Refusing to trust him one minute, and feeling her heart turn to honey the next, at the sight of him on his knees.

She covered her face with her hands.

Lieber Gott, hilfe mich. Help me to know dei Wille for me. If Stephen isn't part of Your will, then show me a path that will take me away from him, because I don't know if I can find it on my own. I

want to push him away, keep my heart safe from being crushed again.
But then he does something to make me wonder if he is a different man
now. A man standing in the circle of Your will. A circle that might be
big enough for two, if only I knew the way to go. Help me, Lord. I
humbly ask in Your Son's name.

She heard the doorknob turn and opened her eyes.

Little Matty stood there, gazing at her, before he trotted over to put a hand on her knee. "Why are you crying, Susanna?"

Her smile was a little wobbly as she lifted him into her lap. "I wasn't. I was talking to the Lord."

"Who's that?"

Well, there was a subject for a whole lifetime. "He's our Father up in heaven. When we talk to Him, and bring our troubles to Him, He can help us."

"Oh." Matty thought this over. "Like Stephen and Adam?"

A chuckle bubbled out of her. "*Ja.* Only He's much bigger. And He loves us enormously. His love can fill the whole sky, all the way up to the stars ... or be right here." She touched his chest.

"That's where Mama's love lives. She told me."

She nodded. "My mama's does, too."

"And Stephen's?"

"He loves his family, and *Gott*. And that love lives right there." She touched his chest again.

"And you?"

She gave him a hug. "And me what?"

"Do you live right there inside Stephen?" He touched her dress, below the collarbone.

Susanna lifted her head just in time to see someone pass the door. The only person whose room lay past hers was his.

Had he heard? Goodness me—out of the mouths of babes and sucklings.

"I'm his friend, *Liewi*," she said at last, since Matty was waiting for an answer. "Our hearts are big enough to hold all our friends. Even Clancy. He's Stephen's horse."

Matty giggled at the picture this made in his mind. "What's *loovee*?"

"That's our word for sweetie. Sometimes we—" Something soft fell against the window, and both Susanna and Matty turned to see what had happened. "Matty, look!"

The snow that pressed up against the window had slumped under its own weight, and a good foot of blue sky now showed above it.

She set him on his feet. "The snow is melting for true. Let's go see if we can shovel our way out the front door."

The snow was still pretty deep, covering the steps to the front porch as though they weren't even there, and drifting in under the overhang the way it had at the back door. Stephen was already at work with the snow shovel he'd brought from the barn, his strokes firm and even.

"It's melting," she said from the door. "Feel how much warmer it is."

"I might have only half a job left by tomorrow," he said by way of agreement.

He cleared four or five of the front stairs, which was a bit like excavating a mountain from the bottom.

"Come on, Matty, let's help," she suggested. "If you take a saucepan, I'll use the canner your mom was using this morning."

The little boy manfully tried to mimic her actions, but even though more snow seemed to fall out of the little pot back onto the porch than fly into the drifts beyond it, she knew better than to dampen his enthusiasm with suggestions or criticism. He was a darling to want to help.

By lunchtime, they had managed to clear the steps.

"Whew," she said, lowering the canner and swiping at her damp face. She gazed at the walls of snow on either side, higher than her head. "No one can get through the yard or up the lane, but if they can fly, they can land on the steps, anyway."

Matty had gone into the house several steps ago, to tell his mother how much he had helped, leaving Suzanna alone with Stephen in the bright sunlight.

"The birds would probably appreciate some seeds, if Sara has any." On the bottom step, he gazed over the drifts that would have come up to his chin if he'd walked out into them. "I wonder how the calves are managing."

"Their mothers will bed down under the pines and keep them warm," she said. "Remember that first winter you were at the Four Winds? That February storm?"

"I was so thankful we'd brought all the pregnant cattle into the home fields. If it hadn't been for the shelter of all the piñon pines we'd have lost many more of the newborns than we did."

There was that word again. *We.*

"Who did you sell the ranch to?" he asked after a moment.

Susanna made a wry face. "Mamm got an offer she couldn't refuse from the celebrity who owns the spread next to ours. That's the only reason we could buy the Inn and renovate it—the money not only paid off the ranch's mortgage, but the Inn's too."

"A blessing," he said. "Twice over."

"Mind you, the owner here was old and had been trying to

sell the property for years, so Mamm got it for a pretty good price."

"It looks right welcoming now. If you meant it about that spaghetti dinner, maybe you could give me a tour."

She turned it into a joke. "Sure—after this, the business's reputation might be ruined and we'll have empty rooms all summer. You can look into as many as you like."

"I doubt that will happen." Leaning on the shovel, he smiled. "But I meant it about the dinner."

Oh, that smile. The one that came so rarely, but how it could play with a girl's heartbeat when it did.

"Stop that." She hefted the wet canner on to one hip.

"Stop what?"

Don't look so innocent. "You know perfectly well. I'm not going to warm up cold soup with you, Stephen. I was just being polite—a sister inviting a brother to dinner as a thank-you."

He nodded, his lips twitching as he tried to do as she said, and failing miserably. "You seem to have forgotten that I really, really like soup. And the only way I plan to be a brother to you is in the Spirit. Consider yourself warned."

That grin could have melted the snow in a circle all around him.

There was only one thing her sense of self-preservation could do. She fled into the house with the canner, the sweet sound of his laughter following her even through the closed door.

14

THERE WAS nothing like stating your intentions right up front. Stephen had given Susanna fair warning. He'd obviously expected her to turn tail and run, and so she had—because what else could she do now that he'd been crystal clear that he aimed to pursue her?

Susanna couldn't face it. *Really, mei Vater? Are You seeking to punish me?*

Even if He wasn't, she couldn't get around the fact that she and Stephen had to get through this experience somehow, and to do that, she'd better walk circumspectly and take care of her heart.

The only saving grace was, the arctic front that had rolled in so fast to put them in this situation seemed to be doing its best now to rectify it. The *plink* of water dripping off the trees, the gurgle of it in the eaves and drainpipes, sounded almost like a tiny symphony, each beat shortening the time this torture would go on.

By late afternoon, the steps they had shoveled off this morning were actually drying in the sun. The walls of snow

143

were still high on either side, but with her experience in mountain winters, she would not be surprised to find them half that height by tomorrow. While she was in the kitchen teaching Zefra how to make meatballs from scratch, Stephen helped Matty make his snowman at the bottom of the steps, warning him that, like Frosty, he might be leaving soon.

The windows were open to admit the warming air, so both she and Zefra heard Matty say, "That's okay, Stephen. We are, too."

She could only hope they could all leave. And soon.

Dinner that night was a triumph. "I wrote down everything we did, step by step," Zefra told Stephen, "so that I could do it when Matty and I are on our own. Though I don't think I can get ground elk to mix in with the beef anywhere but here."

"You can use all hamburger, like most people," Susanna said with a smile. "The secret is in the sauce, and in the oatmeal and egg in the hamburger."

"Two things I never imagined could be in a meatball," Zefra said.

"I like meatballs," Matty said around his food. "They're *goot*."

Susanna burst into laughter, even as Stephen guffawed in appreciation. "If he goes to the Amish school across the road from the Rocking Diamond, he might come home with more *Deitsch* words than English," she said. "Our scholars speak *Deitsch* at home, then learn English at school."

"That's okay," Zefra said. "I took German in high school, and I was sent to Germany for a course by the hotel chain I worked for. There are a lot of similarities. It would be fun to learn some words with him."

"We only educate our *Kinner* up to eighth grade," Stephen warned her. "If you live here long enough, Matty will have to go into Mountain Home to the high school. There might be some subjects our Amish teachers won't cover, as well."

"I figured so," Zefra said equably. "When the time comes, I can tutor him in the pieces that are missing, or find a home-schooling group to help. Between the schoolhouse and the ranch, the important things I want him to learn will be covered."

Susanna glanced at Stephen, and in his thoughtful nod could imagine his memories were much the same as hers, even growing up several states away. Amish children learned more than reading, writing, and arithmetic. Teamwork, not competition, for instance. Putting others before yourself in small things, so that doing so in larger things would not seem so difficult.

"Good deeds have echoes," Grossmammi used to say. It wasn't until Susanna was grown up that she came to understand what that meant. The things you did for others had ramifications, not only in their gratitude, but in the way you were treated, and even in how you were remembered. And it all began in the little one-room *Schulhaus* when a child was barely big enough to see over the teacher's desk.

After dinner, Zefra got up to help Susanna with the dishes. But Stephen got to the dishtowels before her. "You and Matty might need some reading time," he said. "I can look after these. After all, you helped cook."

Zefra didn't need to be told twice. There were still books on the shelf that Matty hadn't seen.

Stephen began to dry the water glasses, pointedly ignoring Susanna's frown. "You didn't have to do that," she said, twisting the dishcloth into a glass. If she wasn't careful, she just might push it right through the bottom.

"I know. But I don't mind helping. You've been doing such

a good job of feeding us that it's only fair I should help with the cleanup."

"We're going to have to restock Sara and Josh's refrigerator and pantry." She let his compliment fly right past her. "If the anglers pay Mamm for the extra days they were forced to stay, I might even be able to afford it."

"They'll pay," he said. "Your mother's meals are worth the price of an extra night or two."

Another reference to the past. Time to change the subject. "Do you think we'll be able to leave in the morning?"

He lifted a shoulder in a shrug, and started on the plates. "If it keeps up like this, your only problem won't be snow. It'll be driving the buggy down the lane without getting stuck in the mud."

"April all over again."

From the sitting room came the sound of Zefra's soft alto voice, reading about a dog named Carl.

"I used to like those books," Susanna said to the soapsuds. "They don't have words, you know. Mamm and Dat used to change the story just a little every time, and Seth would always insist that they read it exactly the same way."

"My sisters, too. I kind of liked it different. I might not know what to expect, but I did know my parents and Carl would make it come out right in the end."

"Me, too. Funny how we trust the reader as much as the story, when we're little."

"I think it's *gut* that we do," he said thoughtfully. "Trust comes from all sorts of places. That's the mistake I made when I left the Four Winds. I broke your trust."

She managed to hang onto the pot she was scrubbing, but even so, a hot wave of color prickled into her cheeks. And unfortunately, she couldn't very well hide it.

"I'm sorry for that, Susanna," he said quietly. "I went riding off to be a knight in shining armor for someone who didn't need one. *Gott* humbled me in the most painful way a man can be humbled, and I deserved it."

"I'm sorry you were hurt," she whispered. It was a small miracle that she could say that honestly. But she had put herself in his shoes more than once in the dark reaches of the night, and tried to imagine how a man would feel to give up his job and prospects to go all that way for nothing ... except a great big helping of humiliation.

"Like I said, I deserved it. God pruned me back so that I could mature in the right way. Grow in my faith the way He wanted. And someday, somehow, be a man who was worthy of you."

"Ach, Stephen," she whispered. "I don't need a knight in shining armor either."

"They're not very practical in ranch life, I agree. Too hard on the horses." He stretched up to put the plates in the cupboard. "But I want to be a better man. The kind that keeps his eyes on what *Gott* puts right in front of him, and not on—" He stopped, as if searching for the right word.

"What He has taken away?"

"Exactly."

Could she do that, too? Goodness knew she had been focused on what she'd lost for so long it had almost become a part of her. That void inside was made of lack. Lack of trust. Lack of faith in him. Lack of hope that it would be any different if the circumstances repeated themselves.

How was a person supposed to turn that void into something productive and functioning?

To let go of the lack and embrace the fullness of the future?

"I won't say any more now." He closed the cupboard on the pots. "I wanted to say how I feel, since I've told you just about everything else I promised myself I wouldn't."

With a smile, he hung the dish towel over its rail on the stove door, and ambled out to the living room to hear the end of Carl's adventure.

What a relief he hadn't said any more. Susanna was the kind who liked company, but sometimes it was necessary for a girl to pull herself together in peace. Later, when she quietly said good night to Stephen after Zefra and Matty had gone to bed, she was thankful when all he said was, "*Guder nacht*. Sleep well."

The quiet of her room was refreshing, despite the continuous gurgle of melting snow. But even though she usually found it easy to fall asleep to the sound of water, tonight it was a little harder. In her dreams, it was the same. She was walking next to a creek through a forest she didn't recognize, the words *worthy of you* sounding in the distance like an echo whose source she was trying to find.

IN THE MORNING, SUSANNA WAS ALMOST AFRAID TO LOOK out the guest room window. But she had to—it was fully clear of snow, which meant the drift that had covered this side of the house had melted down. But how much?

She dared to throw up the old-fashioned sash and lean out.

"Holy smokes."

The air held only the normal coolness of an early summer morning, not the subzero chill they'd been warding off with the woodstove. It was nearly six o'clock and she'd overslept, so the sky was lighter. Over the trees to the west it was pink and lavender, which meant that on the other side of the house, she'd see a golden glow growing in the notch between two mountains.

And the snow—could that be a *fence post* over there? She blinked and looked again. Her eyes had not deceived her. The top of a fence post was exposed. And another, and ... *ja*, for sure and certain that was the top wire of the fence!

What a miracle, to see it had melted that much overnight!

Her steps were light as she went into the kitchen to start the coffee. If she thought that Stephen might have overslept, too, she soon found out he'd done no such thing. One glance out the window in the mudroom door showed him out there with the snow shovel, digging a proper path to the barn.

The walls of snow only came up to his elbows now. And while he hadn't made more than ten feet of progress, it was ten feet that they hadn't been able to manage yesterday. They might just be able to get home today.

Please, mei Vater, let it be so.

When Stephen came in at seven thirty, soaked and red in the face but triumphant, she and Zefra had a fresh pot of coffee ready and breakfast on the table.

"I made the bacon and onion pie," Zefra informed him proudly after the silent grace. She might not be a praying person, but she had already taught Matty to bow his head respectfully when other people did. "Crust and all, can you believe it?"

"It's delicious," Stephen told her, shoveling it in with such an appetite it was a wonder he could taste it at all. After Stephen had fed and watered the animals, he had brought back the eggs to replace what they'd used this morning. Matty had clapped and jumped up and down on the back porch when he'd seen him returning between the walls of snow with his hands full, and had been allowed to help carry them inside.

Susanna had felt like clapping, too. Who knew that the ability to walk to the barn was such a gift?

"Sara has a cookbook on her shelf, and I just followed the instructions, and it worked." From Zefra's tone, this was the second or third miracle of the day. "Susanna made the biscuits, though. That's, like, graduate-level cooking, and I'm only in kindergarten."

Susanna had to laugh. "I think you'll find the recipe in that book, too. If you can make pie crust, you can make biscuits. You've got the knack, Zefra. Don't be afraid to try anything you want to. Just follow the recipe and you'll do great."

"I won't be adding cooking to my job description at the Rocking Diamond anytime soon," she said wryly, "but it's *goot* to know I can feed the two of us with more than hot dogs and macaroni and cheese."

"I'll give you Mamm's recipe for macaroni and cheese," Susanna said. "It will knock your *Schtrimpe* off."

"I'll second that," Stephen said.

Susanna tilted her head toward him for Zefra's benefit, and explained, "He was a big fan."

Zefra shook her head at them. "What does *Schtrimpe* mean?"

"Shrimp!" Matty repeated.

"Not quite," Stephen told him with a grin. "It means socks."

"Oh, like *Strümpfe* in German," Zefra guessed.

"That's what we call *hoch Deutsch*, or high German. *Ja*, it probably comes from that. See? You'll be learning *Deitsch* as easily as cooking pretty soon."

Zefra looked so pleased that Susanna could only hope this

Taylor Madison person at the Rocking Diamond would be as encouraging. It would be such a shame to see that glow extinguished by a demanding employer.

Susanna spent the morning cleaning, just in case they were indeed able to leave in the afternoon. Near lunchtime, she lifted the mop to listen to a growl in the distance.

"Could that be—?"

She and Zefra dashed to the front window just in time to see the county snowplow labor past a quarter mile away, throwing up a fountain of snow as it cleared their side of Dutchman Road.

"I think my car just got buried twice as deep," Zefra sighed in despair.

"Stephen can find it, Mama," Matty said, standing on tiptoe to peer out between them at the fountain of snow in the distance.

"He probably could, baby ... by the weekend. But Mama has to get to our new house sooner than that."

There was a *gut* solution to that dilemma that didn't involve *Englisch* cars at all. "If the snow keeps melting, we could take you in the buggy. Or on horseback."

Zefra's brown eyes widened. "Really?"

"We might have to dig through the snow at the end of the lane where the plow went by, but even if it's too deep for Sal to pull the buggy, we can still get you and Matty there. It isn't far."

"Is Sal trained for riding?" Stephen came through from the mudroom in sock feet, having clearly heard his name. "I've widened the path to the barn and dug out the barn door a bit more. The chickens aren't interested in coming outside."

"I don't blame them," Zefra said fervently. "Watch your feet. Susanna just got done washing that floor."

"Oops," he said, skirting around the edges of the floors to join them at the living-room window. "She's the woman with the mop, and she knows how to use it."

"Only on people who don't take off their boots," Susanna informed him. "Doesn't look like we can get Zefra's bags out of her car, but at least we can get her to the ranch."

"It's above sixty and the thermometer is rising," Stephen said. "Let's see how things look this afternoon."

Susanna and Zefra made certain the house was spotless, all the dishes were done, and even a cheerful note of thanks from all four of them left on the dining table, held down by the salt shaker. And by four o'clock Stephen nodded with satisfaction. "Less than a foot? No problem. Amazing what a difference thirty degrees makes."

They soon found out that eight feet of melted snow going straight into the soil made a number of other differences. Namely ground so soft that without boots like Stephen's, their feet sank into it with a squelch.

"I was afraid of this," Susanna said, retreating to the back porch before she was up to her ankles in mud. "Zefra, have you ever ridden before?"

"The closest I've ever been to a horse is asking directions to a museum from a mounted cop."

"All right," Stephen said. "I'll lay down some boards I found so you can get over to the barn. Then I'll take Matty up with me, and you can go with Susanna on Sal. It'll be bareback, but if you hang on to Susanna, you should be fine for the short distance we have to go."

Stephen headed to the barn, while Zefra hurried into the house and returned in a moment with Matty's current favorite picture book, *A Horse for Our Farm*. Susanna had seen the others in the library—*A Chicken for our Farm* and *A Goat for Our*

Farm. Zefra could draw the connection between its story and the adventure Matty was about to have.

"See, baby? We're going to ride to our new house, just like Jason and Julie do when they get Windy saddled." She opened the book to where the characters were boosting each other up, on their stomachs with legs flailing, trying to get into the saddle without something to stand on. She turned the page to where they accomplished it. "You and Stephen will ride just like this, while Mama and Susanna go on Sal."

"You'll be on *Clancy*," Susanna said, her awed tone indicating what an honor this was. "He's such a *goot* cutting horse that my father rode him, and Stephen rides him, and now you'll ride him. How about that!"

"I can ride a horse?" the child repeated in a wondering tone, one finger on Windy and her riders. "With Stephen?"

"Just as soon as he gets Clancy saddled," Susanna assured him.

"And Mama figures out how to get her sorry self up on Sal's back," Zefra muttered as she put the book away. "Jason and Julie are going to look like pros next to me."

"Here's Stephen," Susanna said as he approached, laying down one old fence board head to toe with the next. "It will be good for Matty to watch Stephen saddle up in the barn. The more familiar it looks, the better. And you and I will have things to climb up on to mount Sal."

They said farewell to the snug little house that had been their shelter all this time, and Susanna locked it. The wood in the stove would gradually burn down, leaving the house pleasantly warm whenever its owners returned.

Once they reached the barn, Matty was agog at the horses and chickens he had been missing out on—though getting too close to hooves and beaks was not on his agenda during this first meeting. For Matty's benefit, Stephen conversed with Clancy as he saddled him, explaining everything he was doing. Then Stephen mounted the horse. He reached down for Matty, Zefra handed him up, and he settled the child in front. Clancy glanced over his shoulder and Matty dared to pat him, taking in the world from this high vantage point.

"There now," Stephen said. "You've made a friend."

Susanna had already put the bridle and reins on Sal. She helped Zefra to mount from one of the rails in the unused cattle pen. "Just walk Sal through the door and I'll roll it closed behind you."

Zefra made a whimpering sound that she swallowed immediately, since her son's eyes were fixed on her with a mixture of fear and admiration. "Tally-ho and all that," she said with quavery bravado.

"A little touch with your heels and remember what I told you about the reins."

Clancy led the way, and Sal was perfectly happy to follow him out into the yard. Susanna rolled the big door closed and used a paddock rail to mount in front of Zefra, who passed her the reins and slid her arms around her waist in a death grip.

And then their little string squelched and sucked its way across the yard, around the house, and down the lane. Earlier, Stephen had made a walkway through the big berm the plow had thrown up, so Stephen motioned to Susanna to lead, since she had been to the Rocking Diamond and he had not. The mile and a half seemed to go by in just minutes, even at a leisurely walk. There was no traffic at all, which left the horses able to choose their footing in the slush. Not until they reached the county highway at the bridge did they see their first car, heading out of Montana at a high rate of speed.

"That's the schoolhouse, there," Susanna said, waving to

the right. "And that's the bridge where my cousin saw a man fly out of a car and go down the bank. She saved his life that night —and wound up marrying his brother."

"Wow," Zefra said. Her grip on Susanna had not slackened one bit.

"And there's the gate of the Rocking Diamond. You can't miss it."

The wrought-iron pair of gates that Alden Stolzfus had made still stood open, and it was clear no one had been down the long lane since the snow had begun to fall. They picked their way through the softening berm and headed up the gentle slope. Susanna had been here twice during the family's stay at the Circle M, and even though she knew what to expect as they rounded the last curve to see the big house like a ship on the hillside, it was an impressive sight with its steeply sloped roof and wide verandas. Old West mixed with New Money. Lots of new money. To one side of the house under the pines were the guest cabins, solid and built of logs, and behind the house lay accommodations for the staff, one of which would be Zefra and Matty's new home.

"Holy castle on the hill, Batman," Zefra muttered.

Susanna didn't know what that meant, but the tone was one she'd used herself the first time she'd seen it.

The front staircase had been shoveled off, and as they approached, people began to come out on to the massive deck. A blond woman in pink ostrich cowboy boots hurried down the stairs.

"Zefra Harris? Is that you?"

"It's me, ma'am," Zefra called. "Sorry I'm late."

"Good grief, I should say so. Where have you been?"

"She saw a light the first night of the storm, Mrs Madison, and brought her son to safety in the house we were taking refuge in." Stephen sat easily in the saddle, Matty in the circle of his arm taking in the woman with the snapping blue eyes.

No one made any move to dismount.

"Whose house?"

"My cousin Joshua Miller's," Susanna said. "Do you remember me? Susanna Miller, at the Wild Rose Amish Inn."

"Oh yes, my not-competition. So you stayed at the hay farm? And who is this?"

Stephen didn't seem bothered by the less than friendly greeting. "I'm Stephen Kurtz, foreman at the Bar K ranch. And this here is Matty Harris."

"But where are your bags? Why are you wearing sandals, Zefra? What is going on?"

Zefra had not released her hold on Susanna. "My car was buried in the blizzard, and got buried again when the plow went by this morning. Everything is still in the trunk. I didn't want to be any later starting work, so we came literally with only the clothes on our backs."

Taylor Madison stared at her.

"Now that's a work ethic," someone up on the deck said to his companion. "You'd never hear *that* in New York."

"Good heavens," Mrs Madison said in disbelief. "We are in the midst of an apocalypse and all you can think about is getting to work on time?"

"I have a child to feed, ma'am," Zefra pointed out calmly. "I don't have the luxury of taking advantage of the apocalypse."

Mrs Madison's mouth fell open, and then, unexpectedly, she laughed. "That's what I like to see. Come rain, snow, sleet, or the apocalypse, the staff at the Rocking Diamond are up to the challenge."

A smattering of applause came from the deck, and Susanna felt the arms around her waist relax just a fraction.

"Do you think you can get down?" she murmured over her shoulder to Zefra.

"Find me a rock or something," the young woman muttered back. "And pray I don't fall on my rear in the mud."

Susanna guided Sal over to the bottom-most flagstone step and Zefra slid off as though she'd done it a hundred times—or maybe seen it done on television. Susanna dismounted as well. And when Zefra reached up and Stephen handed Matty to her, she did it with grace, turning to face her employer with Matty's hand gripped in hers.

Susanna was very glad to see that when Mrs Madison waved her thanks to her and Stephen and turned her gaze to her new domestic assistant, the anger had left her eyes and there was nothing but respect in them.

Zefra thanked Stephen, and Matty tilted his head to look up. "Denkee, Stephen!"

"Clancy and I will see you soon, Matty," Stephen replied.

Zefra pulled Susanna into her arms. "Thank you for saving my life," she choked out.

"You saved your own, with God's help," Susanna whispered into her curls. Then she added, "There are three perfectly healthy Madison boys. You have them dig out your car and bring it home when the snow melts enough. Never give them the upper hand."

Zefra kissed her on the cheek and wiped an errant tear away on her own. "Understood. How do you say *good-bye, my friend* in *Deitsch*?"

"*Hatge, mei freind.*"

Zefra repeated it perfectly. And as Susanna remounted Sal and turned her in Stephen's direction, Zefra and Matty mounted the steps to the big house ... and the start of their new life in the Siksika.

15

THE WILD ROSE AMISH INN

When they reached Mountain Home, Stephen didn't even think of waving farewell and riding on to the Bar K. But all the way through town, as he and Clancy rode beside Sal when there was no traffic, and behind her when there was, Susanna kept glancing at him as though she were waiting for him to leave.

Not today, Liewi. Not ever again.

"Look," he said, pointing to Yoder's Variety Store, with the bridge in view beyond it. "The Yoders are already clearing the parking lot."

She made a sound in her throat that was oddly similar to the scrape of shovels on asphalt. "From the looks of those buried cars all along the highway, I'd say they were a little optimistic about customers today."

"Trust me, in two days they'll have all the customers they want. Once the highway opens and the delivery trucks can get through, that is."

The Yoders were overjoyed to see them—and their horse, Sal. Once Susanna apologized for having to leave the buggy behind for now, it was tempting to stand there in the melting parking lot in the sun and exchange blizzard stories. But Sal knew her business. She nodded her head and pushed Calvin between the shoulder blades in an unmistakeable hint that she was tired of chatter and snow and wanted her dry, comfortable barn.

Calvin laughed and led her away, for once not even making a joke or trying to ride her bareback.

Stephen and Susanna said their farewells to the family and she set off alone across the lot. She only got about six steps when Stephen stopped her. "You're not going to walk home, are you?"

She stared at him as if he were crazy. "Of course. I can see the Inn from here."

"And between you and home is a couple hundred yards of unplowed snow at least a foot deep." Her shoulders slumped in realization. "*Kumm mit.* Clancy can take both of us. He has before."

Oh, that got her. She blushed scarlet at the memories—like the time he'd taken her up behind him and they'd ridden along the Rio Ventana on a warm October day. The aspens had burned bright gold among the pines, the river had whispered like music, and he'd kissed her, the sweetness of it intensifying the beauty all around them.

"I'll be fine."

"You'll be frozen and wet to the knees, and your mamm will scold me for not taking better care of you."

"Stephen, the entire Yoder family is looking at us."

Not a single shovel was scraping and minding its own business.

"Then act natural."

"Great," she grumbled, waiting for him to mount and then

using the stirrup to swing up behind him. "It will be all over the district by suppertime."

"The district," he said as Clancy responded to his knees and heels, "has far more interesting things to talk about. *Where were you during the blizzard* will be the only subject at every dinner table from now until the fourth of July."

How naturally her hands went around his waist—and Clancy seemed to recognize her familiar weight as well. As they made the turn into Creekside Lane, the horse was up to his knees, too, but the snow was so soft and melting that there was no danger of shards of ice tearing up his legs. Susanna slid off the moment Stephen brought him to a halt at the Inn's gate, and by the time she got it open, the whole household had poured out into the neatly shoveled parking lot.

"Susanna!" Rachel shrieked, snatching her daughter up in her arms in such a bear hug Stephen wondered how either of them could breathe. But they spoke, in broken, joyful snatches of question and answer so quick he could hardly keep up.

Then Rachel's teary-eyed gaze found him just as he was thinking he probably ought to go.

"Stephen, how can I ever thank you for looking after my girl?"

He swung down from the saddle and barely braced himself in time for the strength of Rachel's hug. "She looked after us, more like. She taught Zefra how to cook—"

"And you taught Matty how to ride—" Susanna put in.

"And both of us taught them a few words of *Deitsch*," he finished. "We all looked after each other."

"Are Seth and Gideon still at the Circle M?" Susanna wanted to know.

"*Ja*—no point in their struggling to get back here," Rachel said. "They'll have plenty to do once the snow melts. They need to ride up on the allotment."

So did Stephen. But that was work for tomorrow. He still had today. And Susanna.

"And Tobias?" Susanna looked anxious. "Have you heard?"

"Josiah Keim just called to find out if we'd heard from you today. Tobias is there. Apparently it's quite a story. I'm not sure I want to hear it—all the twins and I need to know is that he's safe."

Susanna's eyes closed briefly in a way that instantly told Stephen she was thanking *der Herr* for His mercy.

"Stephen, you'll come in for something to eat? And to meet our guests?"

A small group of *Englisch* folks hung back by the porch stairs, as though uncertain whether they ought to intrude on the family reunion.

He felt as though the Millers were family. More than simply his former employers. He'd come to love them, to count Tobias, Gideon, and Seth almost as brothers. And after being so close to Susanna for three days and two nights, he simply wasn't capable of mounting Clancy and riding out of that gate. Besides, another hour of sunshine would only melt the snow more, and make the ride easier.

"I'd like that," he said, and led Clancy over to the hitching rail by the brick patio, where half a bale of hay waited for any Amish animals who needed it. The Inn's fluffy gold chicken was sitting on top of it, and got pretty huffy when Clancy asked her to move.

The two ladies on the porch laughed and took pictures of Clancy, nose to beak with the indignant bird, while her chicks fled to the safety of the melted-off patio.

Somehow what he'd expected to be coffee and cake

turned out to be supper—the most delicious chicken and dumpling stew Stephen had smelled since he'd left the Four Winds. His nose even detected the hint of green chile among the herbs and vegetables—Rachel's special touch. The *Englisch* guests waited respectfully for their hosts to say the silent grace, as though it had become something they not only expected, but respected. The dumplings were like clouds melting in his mouth, the potatoes ran with butter, and he was informed that the carrots in dill sauce were the last ones in the house.

"If we don't get to the grocery store tomorrow," Rachel predicted, "it'll be oatmeal and pickles for all three meals."

"I'd eat oatmeal with your pickles any time," said one of the fishermen around a big bite of dumpling.

"When we get back, I swear I'm going to start my novel," one of his companions said. "It'll open with four guys coming to Montana to fish, and being snowed in with an Amish family."

"They all gain twenty pounds and live happily ever after," said one of the ladies with a laugh. Sandra, her name was.

"Pretty much," the man said, smiling into his stew. "It'll be a bestseller."

Dessert was snitz pie with cream poured over it, and Stephen wondered if he would burst the seams in his pants when he mounted Clancy. His employer's wife Kathryn was a *gut* cook, and she'd taught her daughter well, but Rachel had a gift for putting a little extra twist in things. Susanna was like that, too. And while a man didn't love a woman for her cooking, it—

Stephen felt a tingle run over him from his scalp to his feet.

Love.

His forkful of pie had halted in midair, and it was all he could do to get it to his mouth in some way close to normal.

Because he didn't feel normal. He felt as though the world had stopped, just for a second, and then begun spinning at a different speed. He'd been *in love* with Susanna, but a man who truly *loved* would never have galloped off to Colorado and left her the way he had. A man who loved Susanna Miller the way she deserved to be loved would stay by her side through thick and thin. Through blizzard and bounty. Even if all they had was pickles and oatmeal, he'd eat them and be grateful, simply because her hands had made them.

His mind reeled. It was one thing to make a decision to court a woman. Even if it was the second time. It was quite another to realize that loving her meant yielding her the freedom to choose him ... or someone else. Even if she didn't choose him, when all was said and done, he would still love her. He was stepping out in faith, on the knowledge that *Gott* had brought him back to the valley for one purpose: to love Susanna. He would hold to that, hold to his heart's promise to her, and somehow, some way, the Lord would turn her steps to him even as He'd turned Stephen's steps to her.

"...isn't that right, Stephen?"

He blinked at little Gracie, who with her twin, was well enough now to sit at the table with them, even if she was still hoarse.

"What's that?" He had no idea what anyone was talking about. The flow of conversation had eddied right around the towering rock of his realization.

Gracie looked at him and made a face. "I said, you're coming to help with the barn raising, aren't you? It's on Tuesday."

"Gracie," Rachel said in a tone that meant they'd had this

discussion several times already, "they're only pouring the foundation Tuesday. The actual raising is the Tuesday after." She looked over at Stephen. "At least, I hope it is. I don't know if the concrete truck can even get into the field, never mind out again. We might have to move the whole project later in the summer."

"Mammi," Benny groaned. "We can't see our horses yet? It's been *years*."

Stephen thought it better to stick to the point when he replied to the child. "I'm not sure I could come as soon as Tuesday anyhow, Gracie. A lot of the ranchers will be up on the allotments, checking to make sure the calves survived the blizzard. I know I will. So will your cousins on the Circle M."

"Given a choice between a barn and little calves who need help, which would you pick?" the lady called Merrill asked solemnly.

"The calves," Gracie said at once. "I don't want any of them to die."

Stephen nodded. "Neither do I. But I promise that once we know they're all right, all of us will be there to help with the barn raising."

"Dat said I was old enough to hammer nails," Benny informed his sister. "*You* have to stay with the *Bopplin*."

Gracie's eyes filled with tears at this set-down.

Rachel said smoothly, "Don't be so sure, Benjamin Miller. People are coming to help us out of love and kindness. The least we can do is serve them in return. Gracie and Susanna will be helping me to make our brothers and sisters feel welcome. It will be a lot of work for everyone, both in the barn and outside. Your sister has a very important part, pouring water and lemonade for thirsty men, filling plates, and making certain all our helpers have what they need."

Gracie tilted her chin at her twin in a way that clearly said, *So there.*

Benny was not a stupid boy. He could see that antagonizing the person who could take away his plate before he was finished was not very smart.

"I guess feeding everyone who comes is as important as banging nails," he conceded.

"A barn doesn't get built without both," Stephen agreed.

He glanced at Susanna, who smiled at him with her eyes, the way they used to at the big ranch table on the Four Winds, having entire conversations and creating inside jokes without saying a word.

He could see the moment when she remembered, too. She dropped her gaze to her plate. It was all too telling that communicating this way came easily to them. Instinctively, almost. And every time it happened, he hoped it would remind her that while he was part of her past, he wanted to be her future even more.

❧

STEPHEN HAD RIDDEN OFF IN THE TWILIGHT ON CLANCY, and the twins had gone reluctantly to bed after talking to their father on the cell phone and assuring him that Susanna was home and safe. The lady anglers had also gone to bed, taking a couple of books from the sitting room to read, while the fishermen were still in there, combing the Internet on their phones for news of the highway being opened sometime this month. Their voices came in a low murmur as Susanna snuggled against her mother's side on the old sofa in the family sitting room.

"It's so good to be home," she sighed.

"The Inn is feeling like home after only a few months?"

She nodded. "This sofa never changes, and my bed is my own. I still smell sage in the towels in the bathroom, just like we did at the Four Winds. But most of all, even with half of us missing at the moment, our family is here."

"And Stephen is here."

Susanna felt a jolt in her stomach. She must have stiffened, because Mamm slipped an arm around her shoulders and gave her a gentle squeeze. "The whole valley knows you were snowed in together. I hope you're prepared for some teasing."

"If it's only teasing, I'll be glad. You don't think that people will ... make remarks about us being alone there overnight, do you?"

Rachel lifted a shoulder in a shrug. "If they do, it's a sign that they don't trust themselves in a similar situation. Because you were only alone for a few hours, if I heard the story right. Then that *Englisch* woman and her son came in from the storm."

"Zefra. And Matty. He's completely adorable, and even in such a short time, she became a *gut* friend."

"Adversity can certainly do that. Bring people together in ways that nothing else can. What about you and Stephen? Did you become *gut* friends again?"

Had they? In some ways, it was almost as though they'd never been apart. And in others ... "Ach, Mamm, we had the most awful fight."

"You were frightened. And fear can make people attack each other."

"No, it wasn't like that. I didn't feel afraid at all. Not with him there. It was—" Was she betraying a confidence? How would she feel in Lena Schrock's place?

Mamm sat quietly, waiting. In the other room, one of the fishermen groaned. Maybe the weather report was bad.

Not so long ago, Susanna had promised her mother that there would be no more secrets between them. She made up her mind. "We fought about why he left the Four Winds."

"Did he tell you the reason? I know it has been troubling you for months."

"Yes, after I needled and prodded and picked until he finally blew up. We—we *shouted* at each other." A blush flooded into her cheeks. Well, she *should* be ashamed of herself. It was a wonder Stephen hadn't decided to take his chances with the weather and marched right out the door.

"Strong feelings can make a person do that," Mamm said mildly. "Did you apologize afterward?"

"*Ja*, and then it all came out. This girl, Lena Schrock—"

"From the family he's such good friends with in Colorado?"

How did Mamm remember these things? "The same. Well, she was *im e familye weg.* I was convinced— I mean, I accused him of—"

"Ach, Susanna."

She buried her face in Mamm's shoulder. "I know." Her voice was muffled. Then she took a breath and straightened up a little. "Needless to say, I was wrong. She had been seeing a fence jumper who refused to have anything to do with her or the baby. Her family disowned her, and she was put under the *bann*."

Mamm's fingers went to her lips.

"That's when she contacted Stephen, at her wits' end. He collected his pay, trailered Clancy, and rode off to Colorado to help. Or rather, to ask her to marry him and let him be the baby's father."

Now she felt the jolt of surprise in Mamm's body. "Gracious. I take it she said no?"

Susanna nodded. "She told him she didn't need a knight in shining armor. But I think she just didn't want an Amish man. The last he heard, she had married an *Englisch* man, and he doesn't believe her parents will ever meet their grandson."

"How horribly sad. I can't imagine putting Gracie and Benny out of my life, no matter what Tobias might do."

Susanna couldn't, either. But every family was different. Stephen's, too.

"So we moved here," she went on, "and he got work on the Bar K, and the next thing you know, we're in the same valley, the same church district, and as of three days ago, snowed into the same *Haus*."

"Seems like *der gut Gott* has been busy on your behalf, *Liewi*."

Susanna frowned. "What do you mean?"

"You said it yourself. *Gott* has been drawing the two of you together in the same way He drew Luke and me together. Once you see the pattern, the *wunderbaar*, beautifully designed pattern, you can't unsee it. You can only accept it. And give thanks for it."

Susanna pushed herself upright. "But he left me, Mamm! After all the dreams we had, all that had gone on between us, Lena Schrock just had to crook her finger and he came running. *And he never planned to come back.* That's the part that I just can't get past. He planned to marry someone else who didn't even love him, leaving the one who *did* love him behind."

"It was noble and foolish and unnecessary, I agree."

"It was cruel! And even more cruel is coming back and

acting like all he has to do is crook his finger and *I'll* come running!"

"Do you really think he feels that?"

She slumped against the sofa cushions, her arms crossed. "I don't know. Maybe not. Maybe my pride is hurt as much as my heart."

"Pride heals more quickly than hearts, I have to say. So you don't care for him any more? Is the wound too deep for healing?"

"It would be if I didn't sort of understand what made him do it. His family, you know ... they're not like us. Not close. I think that when the Schrocks took him in when he was sixteen, they became his family. That when he went galloping off to Lena, it was more like a brother coming to the rescue of a sister in trouble than a man traveling all that way to be with the woman he loved."

"A lifetime married to someone he thought of as a sister would be ... difficult." Susanna could hear the restraint in her mother's tone, as though there were a whole lot of other things she'd like to say.

"But there was the *Boppli*, too."

"Who has a father now, from what you say."

Susanna could feel her mother's gaze on her. The passionate energy with which she'd just spoken was rapidly draining away.

"I don't know what I feel, Mamm. He keeps drawing me in, the way he always did. But what if I let myself love him and someone else needs to be rescued? What if he leaves again?"

"I think he might have learned his lesson, don't you? And maybe he's seen the pattern in *Gott*'s design, too."

"Maybe." She hugged her mother and got up. "And maybe I need to sleep on all this in my own bed."

"Don't be afraid to ask for help," Mamm suggested with a smile. "Maybe the One who has arranged it might show you what He's up to yet."

❧ 16 ❧

THE CIRCLE M RANCH

Monday, June 6

BY SATURDAY, all that remained to tell the blizzard's tale were the heaps of snow on the sides of the highway, and even they were melting fast into the deep roadside ditches. The creek at the bottom of the Inn's lawn was running higher than usual with all the snowmelt, and to the valley's relief, the county highway had finally opened. This meant that Sara and Joshua and Nathan Miller could return at last, so on Monday, the entire Miller family gathered at the Circle M for dinner and a good long visit.

"Jimmy the taxi-van driver couldn't unload us fast enough," Joshua said with a laugh. "Good thing we aren't easily offended."

"He was as crazy to get home as we were," Sara said, cuddling Nathan as the Miller women got the massive meal on the table. "I couldn't blame him. What an ordeal you've all had while we've been living the high life in Libby!"

The silent grace was a little longer than usual—they all had a lot to be thankful for. When Susanna raised her head, she took in her brothers one at a time. Tobias, seated between his *Kinner*, his eyes gentle as he touched Gracie's hair or squeezed Benny's shoulders. Seth and Gideon, who along with Adam, Zach, and Reuben, had been riding the allotments for a couple of days now, tracking down and counting calves. They had come back to observe the Lord's day and enjoy this family reunion today. Tomorrow, they'd all be saddling up before daybreak to ride out on the mountains again.

So would Stephen. She hadn't heard from him and hadn't really expected to. He had work to do, and the lives of the calves were important.

But still ...

Her mother and Naomi gazed over the long, crowded table, and Susanna could practically see that the prayers of thanksgiving were still echoing in their minds as they began to pass the food. The two of them, along with Malena, Rebecca King, Kate Weaver, and Lovina Miller, had produced a celebratory feast. There hadn't been time for a trip to their rented freezer in Mountain Home to collect elk meat for Naomi's famous stew, but from the four Miller kitchens came a pot luck meal fit for a king.

Naomi had made poppyseed chicken, Lovina a green bean and sausage casserole straight from her mother's Lancaster County cookbook. Sara had contributed lasagna, and Rachel and Susanna had brought a roasted sweet potato casserole and two big salads, since luckily the trucks had come to supply the grocery store in town. With four different kinds of pickles and fresh-made bread, it was a wonder their stomachs could hold half of it. And dessert waited yet on the kitchen counters—a big German chocolate cake and several rhubarb crumb pies.

"I'm glad to see you're looking all right, Susanna," Adam

said cheerfully. "How many times did you have to take the flying carpet over to the barn?"

"Flying carpet!" Benny exclaimed. "How did you get it to fly?"

Adam laughed and explained how he and Stephen Kurtz had crossed the yard to get to the animals that morning.

"I was never so glad to see anyone," Susanna said fervently. "I was the one who felt like she was flying when you slid through that hole and right in the door."

"Oh, I bet you were pretty glad to see Stephen," Gideon said with a knowing smirk.

"Not at first," she admitted, resisting the urge to stick out her tongue at the big *druwwel-macher*. "But when that diesel rig nearly killed both of us *and* the horses, and we were forced to take refuge in Josh and Sara's house, I was pretty glad he was the one slogging out to get firewood and see to the animals, not me."

Amid the laughter, Sara said, "The house was so clean when we got home I thought we'd come to the wrong place."

"Never mind," Joshua said with a gentle bump of his shoulder on hers. "You left it spotless. Like you knew we were going to have unexpected company."

"All the snow coming in with Zefra and Matty really helped with washing the floor," Susanna went on with bright enthusiasm. "And Adam brought in more at the back, so I didn't even have to fill the bucket to do the kitchen. Just squirt a little soap on it."

When the laughter died down, Kate Weaver asked, "How are your two new friends? I've been trying to think of an excuse to go over to the Rocking Diamond so I can meet Zefra."

"I haven't heard since we took her over there Thursday,"

Susanna said, "but I promised her another cooking lesson. Maybe you can come with me then."

"The car near the end of our lane is gone," Sara said. "So it sounds like she took your advice and browbeat those Madison boys into doing something useful."

"That's *gut* news," Susanna said, pleased. "It's always best to start as you mean to go on. She seems quiet and not one to put herself forward, though."

"She wouldn't have got a job with Taylor Madison unless she had some gumption," Reuben pointed out.

"And Marina is available to train her," Naomi said. "I predict there will be a few additional lessons shared after hours in the management of Madisons."

Zachary helped himself to more lasagna and passed the pan to Ruby Wengerd, his fiancée, sitting beside him. "But now I want to hear how you managed, Tobias," he said. "I can't get a word out of Seth and Gid."

"That's because we don't know," Susanna's brothers chorused. Seth went on, "He promised he'd tell us when he got back."

"Come on, Tobias," Adam urged. "You didn't spend three nights freezing in a haystack, that's for sure and certain."

Tobias grinned. "*Neh*, I didn't, or you'd be talking to an icicle right now and not a man." He took a fortifying bite of green bean casserole and appeared to be arranging facts in his head. "While Susanna took the buggy over to Josh and Sara's for the cough medicine, and Gid and Seth were working here, and Mamm had her hands full with my *kranke Kinner* and all the guests—"

"Who have gone home now," Rachel put in, "with quite a story to tell."

"We're waiting for Alison to tell us what kind of reviews they put up on Help," Susanna added.

"You mean Yelp," Sara said.

"—I had a *delivery*." Tobias pretended to frown at the interruptions, but his eyes twinkled. "Or rather, three deliveries to make, the last one way out on Mountain View Road."

Adam and Zach looked at each other. "That's about as far as you can go before you run into the mountains," the latter said. "It's a long way for the horse."

"It is. And when it started to snow, it got even longer, because I'd gone to the farthest place first. Almost ten miles out, and the ranches are big and far apart. So I tried to hurry Lucky, who turned out to live up to his name. Jason, who owns the feed store and, it turns out, is an ex-Amish man from Lancaster County, sent me out with the Belgian instead of the buggy horse, because the wagon was loaded. Two hundred pounds of poultry feed, a three-phase well pump motor that weighed about the same, and six Japanese maple seedlings."

"My goodness," Lovina said, handing Daniel the poppyseed chicken. "The poultry feed would have made a load just by itself."

"Japanese maples?" Kate wondered aloud. "In Montana?"

"I was glad the feed went first, to the place in the foothills, because wet feed is no joke," Tobias said, nodding. "So Lucky and I were trying to hurry, but even then I think we both knew it was going to get ugly. I still had three miles to go to reach the second place—where the motor was going—when the snow started coming down so hard that I could barely see. And before I'd gone another mile, the wagon got stuck."

"What did you do?" Benny asked, wide-eyed.

"Well, by then it was a foot deep and the temperature was dropping and only a crazy person would keep an animal out in a storm like that no matter how long it lasted. A pickup truck had already slid past me into the ditch. Luckily the man driving was unhurt, and not far from home. So I unhitched Lucky and was about to climb on the wagon to get up on his back, when I remembered the Japanese maples."

His audience stared at him. Only Gracie demanded, "Why, Dat?"

"Because they were some rare breed that had been special ordered. The temperature was already getting pretty crisp, and I knew if I left them and rode to find shelter, they wouldn't survive the night."

"Better them than you," Reuben muttered.

"And replacements would come out of my paycheck to the tune of a hundred dollars apiece."

Benny frowned, trying to do the addition in his head.

"So what did you do?" Susanna asked, half amused by the predicament and half horrified that her brother had been out in that storm when by then, she had found both safety and warmth. And Stephen, but Adam had already regaled the family with the story of his snowshoe trek to find them.

Tobias resumed his tale. "So I decided I would leave the motor and the wagon, because cold wouldn't bother them, and try to get the seedlings and Lucky to safety."

"You took *six trees* with you?" It was the longest sentence Ruby Wengerd had uttered all afternoon. She wasn't much of a talker, especially in a crowd.

"They were only this big." Tobias held a hand about two feet off the checked oilcloth on the table. "They were in little burlap bags full of dirt, so they were kind of heavy. But there was some rope in the wagon, so I tied each pair together and slung one pair over each shoulder and one around my neck, and put the blanket from the wagon around my shoulders to cover them up. All I could hope was that Lucky wouldn't take long to find shelter."

"Which he did." But Seth sounded as if he was leaving it open-ended, despite the clear proof of his brother's survival.

"I thought I was heading for the customer that ordered the pump motor. I meant to tell him where it was, and ask if I could shelter with them. But I got turned around in the white-out, and Lucky was having a harder and harder time getting through the drifts—as though we'd wound up somehow in a field, though with fences that wasn't likely. Not that I could see a fence. It felt like I was in one of those snow globes, with nothing but flakes whirling around me, blotting out every land-mark, every road, even the trees, until I got right up in them. I thought I was heading up the mountain by mistake—which was when I started to pray."

Mamm's face had turned pale.

"Lucky kept going—maybe he has some instinct for shelter that didn't fail him even when mine did. We struggled up over a hill, and that's when I saw a light."

"Just like Zefra," Susanna exclaimed. "We'd put the light in the front window in case people left their cars and were trying to walk to shelter."

Her brother nodded. "So had these folks. And you'll never guess whose ranch it was."

"Keims'," Reuben and Naomi said together. Then Reuben went on, "Sounds like you found your way onto the green belt that runs behind the neurology clinic. The Bar K is on the other side of it."

"I didn't know whose place it was until Lucky and I plowed our way through their yard to the barn. The drifts were halfway to his chest by then. Josiah saw us and came out in boots and hip waders. He got Lucky curried down and comfortable while I got those silly trees unslung from around me and put them in the tack room. You should have seen Josiah's face when he saw that little red forest emerge from under that old wool blanket."

"They were all okay?" Gracie wanted to know.

"Only one branch was broken," he said, giving her a one-armed squeeze. "And when I took them to the customer Saturday, and explained what happened, the lady gave me a fifty-dollar tip for taking such *gut* care of them."

Susanna had to laugh. "Only you would practically risk your life for baby trees."

He smiled back. "That's the thing about any baby. You want to help them. Ask any of these men why they're out on that mountain day in and day out, counting calves. It's not just because of the financial investment, is it?"

"Not entirely," Reuben said, nodding. "So you spent the whole blizzard there at Keims'?"

"*Ja.* I called Mamm as soon as I could, only to be told that Susanna was missing. Then when Stephen didn't come back from dropping off the saddle, things got pretty tense. A lot of praying was going on in every room in the house."

Susanna gazed at him, a dozen questions on the tip of her tongue. Not about Stephen. He had been safe and warm, too—the worst he had to deal with had been a woman shouting at him. No, she was dying to know about Sylvia, and how she felt about being snowed in with Tobias. Not alone, mind you. There had been her cousins Bethany and Sharon, and her parents, and the other hired hands, so the house would have been full.

Had she found the courage to speak? Susanna doubted it. There had been nothing in Tobias's story that had included her. Then again, it wasn't the kind of thing you brought up in front of your entire family. But Susanna would have given a lot to know what had happened in the quiet places in that house —if there had been any. If Tobias had even the smallest clue that his being there was probably the most incredible gift Sylvia Keim had ever received.

But she kept her questions to herself. Because if she asked even one of them, Tobias would waste no time in turning the family's attention to Susanna's being snowed in with her ex for three days.

And nothing in the world would make her talk about *that* to anyone but Mamm.

Tuesday, June 7
The Keim allotment

Chasing calves on a mountainside still wet and treacherous from snowmelt was no joke. Even Clancy, the most sure-footed horse Stephen had ever partnered with, slid down into a draw to rescue a calf stuck in the mud, and then a second time when a chunk of mountainside came loose under his hooves. He had a good sense of balance, though—and luckily, so did Stephen. When it came to roping bawling calves who didn't understand where their mothers had gone, Clancy was a champ, and they made a good team. Even when it involved getting under the panicked calf and pushing while Clancy pulled.

After days of brutal work, they were down to two missing calves and one deceased one, of the thirty-eight that had been turned out. As foreman, it was his job and that of Mark Steiner, the next most senior hand, to find the missing two by hook or by crook. And hope that they were still alive and uninjured.

Today, he realized, was the day the foundation was to be

poured for the barn at the Wild Rose Amish Inn. Any thoughts he might have had of stopping by to check the proceedings and see Susanna had to be set aside. The last two calves were somewhere out there, and he had to find them before coyotes or accident claimed them.

By nightfall, he'd gone farther up on the allotment than he'd ever been, and Mark had taken the one calf they'd found huddling under a big pine down to a bawling cow who was clearly its mother. He whistled and called, to no avail. If he were *Englisch* and this were the celebrity's ranch next door to the Four Winds, he could have called a pilot and boarded a single-engine plane to fly over the territory. But this was an Amish outfit, and while any rancher might have seen such a plane going overhead, it would never occur to any of them to hire one. Men and horses had got the job done for a couple hundred years, Josiah had said to him not long ago, and they'd get the job done now.

Clancy perked up his ears and turned his head.

"All right, partner. Let's see what's over there."

They crested a rocky outcropping and looked over to see a calf bedded down in the grass at the bottom. Stephen felt a stab of anxiety. Had it gone over the edge in a fall of ten feet? Or had it somehow got itself down there and couldn't find the way out?

He guided Clancy around and down the slope. It took some doing, because once it found what it considered safety, the calf wasn't about to leave it. But Clancy at the end of a rope was pretty persuasive, and another hour found them down at the collection pen, where two cows were circling anxiously. Stephen released the calf into their care, and the tenor of the bawling changed to the contented sound of safety and belonging.

"That's all thirty-eight accounted for," he told Mark. "I'm glad the little guy was okay. It would be a sad ending to have found him being the guest of honor at a coyote dinner."

"Bad enough we lost one to start with," Mark said. "Speaking of dinner, what are the chances of getting any, do you suppose?"

"One hundred percent," Stephen assured him with a laugh as they made their way down the trail one behind the other. "Kathryn Keim would never let us go hungry no matter how late we got in."

"Neither would Sylvia," Mark said, as though somehow Stephen had left her out on purpose.

"That's true," he agreed. "I can't imagine any rancher's daughter leaving a couple of hungry hands to themselves."

A few minutes later they arrived at the allotment gate, so he dismounted to open it and let Mark ride through. He closed it securely, and now they could pick up their pace—or rather, the horses made that decision for them. After a long, muddy day, a warm barn, a good rubdown, and a scoop of oats waited, and both animals knew it.

"Do you think she's seeing anybody?" Mark asked out of nowhere.

Stephen's thoughts had drifted back to the rancher's daughter who seemed to take up most of the space in his head, so it took a second to realize Mark had asked him a question. "Who?"

"Sylvia, of course. She's a year or two older than me, but she's sure nice, and she can cook like nobody's business."

Mark might be the next most senior man on the crew, but like Stephen, Josiah had him figured in experience, not time. He'd arrived only a week or two before Stephen himself. But a week or two was enough time to look around and take notice, if a man was of a mind to do that.

"I don't know," he confessed over his shoulder. They had to ride single file along the road now for about a mile, in the wayside path. "I can't recall seeing her talking to anyone in particular at singing, but then, I've only been to one or two since I've been here. You could ask Sharon or Bethany, in private."

Mark snorted. "That would be like asking a radio not to broadcast the weather. Has she driven home with anybody that you noticed?"

He resisted the urge to ask, Who? a second time. "Not that I've seen."

"You're not much help, boss."

"I've been kind of preoccupied with not dying in a blizzard, and calves, and learning the names of a couple dozen families. You'll have to forgive me. In a year I'll do better."

"I don't know if I have a year. Someone is bound to snap her up. And that Susanna Miller, too. Why isn't she married?"

Something jolted from Stephen's heart down through his stomach at her name in another man's mouth. "Which woman do you have your eye on? Make up your mind."

"I know Sylvia better, of course, but Susanna sure is pretty. You know *her* a lot better than most of us—especially after getting snowed in with her."

"Her and an *Englisch* single mother and a four-year-old."

"But you worked for her family. What's she like?"

It took all the self-control Stephen possessed not to inform Mark that she was off the marriage market and he should focus his attention on somebody else. But until things were settled between him and Susanna, he couldn't be presumptuous and say anything of the sort.

"She's kind, and a great cook, and can rope a cow with the best of us."

Mark laughed, and they guided the horses across the road and through the first of the Keim gates. "I'd buy a ticket to see that."

"Well, if we lose any of the hands before roundup in the fall, you just might get a free showing. I hear the girls on the Circle M are pretty handy with a rope, too. And you should see Susanna's *Mamm*—she can cut a calf out of a herd like a quilter with a pair of scissors."

"So is Susanna seeing anyone?"

Stephen decided to walk the fine line of truth. "I heard so, *ja*."

"Who?"

"She doesn't talk about him, but I think there are feelings there."

Mark's shoulders slumped just a little as he rode up beside him. "Well, you'd know."

"I suppose so. But Susanna doesn't hold much back. If she has feelings for something or someone, it usually doesn't take long before she shows it."

"And she's showing it?"

"From what I've seen, *ja*, I'd say so."

"Ah well. Sylvia is still my first choice, and I've got the advantage of working on their place. Now all I have to do is make sure the other guys don't come around. I got a bit worried about Tobias Miller."

"Tobias?" Stephen said in surprise. "What makes you say that?"

"Oh, I don't know. She's nervous around him. And with women, that usually means something."

Stephen shook his head. "Tobias is a dead end. I lived at

the Four Winds, and in all that time I never saw him go a-courting. He's never gotten over losing his wife. She died when the twins were barely out of diapers."

This looked like the best news Mark had had all day—after finding the last two calves. "You don't say. Well, I'm sorry for the man, in that case. Maybe she was just worried about what people would think, him taking shelter in a house where a single woman lived."

"Nobody is going to think twice about that. Especially not Josiah Keim's house. Hey, get the gate, will you? Only two more to go."

Thankfully, Mark was happy to talk about Sylvia, and speculate aloud about whether she might agree to go home with him after singing on Sunday. Stephen was happy to let him talk. The farther the man stayed from the subject of Susanna Miller, the happier Stephen would be.

THE WILD ROSE AMISH INN

Wednesday, June 8

A SHABBY *ENGLISCH* car pulled into the Inn's parking lot as Susanna was dusting the sitting room and organizing the books before the weekend's first set of guests arrived on Friday. She lowered the duster and frowned out the window at the shape of a person in the driver's seat. Their head was bowed as if in prayer, but she knew the person was probably checking email or placing a call. She wasn't expecting anyone to check in this afternoon, but Room One was available until Friday morning if they wanted it.

Or maybe the person was just sightseeing, and the parking lot was a handy place to pull off the road. To be on the safe side, Susanna hurried into the kitchen and piled some peanut butter oatmeal cookies on a plate, then made sure the twins hadn't drained the pitcher of strawberry lemonade while she wasn't looking. Tobias had taken them over to the feed store to keep him company on a delivery, much to their delight, and Mamm had walked up the creek to their Zook cousins' house to buy a wheel of cheese. Luke would be coming back with her for dinner.

The doorbell rang and Susanna hurried to answer it, checking the straight pins in her *Kapp* and smoothing her kitchen apron. She opened the door with a smile of welcome.

The woman on the wide porch smiled back. A baby carrier hung from one hand, in it a baby who wasn't very old, sound asleep. "My phone was right," she said in *Deitsch* as she took in Susanna's clothes. "This is definitely the Amish Inn."

Susanna's smile faltered, then reasserted itself. "Truth in advertising," she said in *Deitsch*, and stood back to let the young woman in. "*Kumm inne*. Are you looking for a room?"

"Well, I'm actually looking for a person, but it's getting late in the day. When I saw the signage on the fence, I thought, what better place to find someone Amish than a place run by the Amish? They'll know, and it will save me a lot of driving around."

Susanna led her into the guest dining room. "Put the baby down, if you like, and help yourself to a cookie. I'll get some lemonade. You're lucky—we have one queen-sized room left, but only until Friday morning. Check-out is at eleven."

"I likely won't need it that long. Just a place to rest for the night. It's been a long drive."

She set the carrier on the floor and slid onto one of the dining room chairs with a sigh. Susanna brought two glasses of strawberry lemonade and joined her. Her curiosity was burning like a candle—the young mother had obviously once been Amish. And a wedding ring had once rested on the fourth finger of her left hand, but all that remained now was a band of paler skin. Could she be a widow, left with a child so young? Then who was this man she was looking for?

Stop making things up. It's none of your business.

"Where have you come from?" she asked, helping herself to a cookie.

"Monte Vista, Colorado. Have you ever been there?"

"*Neh*, not yet. I grew up in New Mexico—the Ventana Valley."

The woman straightened in her chair and took a cookie. "Close."

"Give or take a few hundred miles," Susanna said with a smile. In the western states, distances were so great between Amish communities that they calculated miles in hundreds or by hours on the train. "But so many people left that eventually our community disbanded altogether. So we sold our ranch and moved here. My mother bought the Inn last winter, and after almost completely renovating it, we moved in and opened for business last month."

"I used to know someone in the Ventana Valley."

"Oh? Who? We were a small community. Only one church district. So I would have known them."

"A man called Stephen Kurtz."

Susanna froze. She forced herself to take a breath. Luckily, the baby stirred and stretched, and distracted the woman.

"He was our ranch foreman. He works here now—on Josiah and Kathryn Keim's place over to the northeast." Susanna waved a hand in that direction, hoping her guest didn't see it tremble. "I'm sorry—I didn't catch your name. I'm Susanna Miller."

The woman smiled. "I know. I read it on your website. I'm Lena Schrock. Or I was. My married name is Johnson."

Susanna had once been butted in the stomach by a panicked calf. It had knocked her to the ground, and she'd lain there gasping for breath until her lungs would work again. It felt a little like that now.

Breathe in. Out. Take another breath. Gut. Now another.

"Stephen has spoken of you," she said when she was able to speak. How amazing that her voice was so calm. "He worked for your family when he was a young man, didn't he?"

"*Ja*, he did. He was my best friend." Lena made a sound in her throat and shook her head ruefully. "Funny how you don't realize the value of best friends. And when we start dating and looking for a *gut* husband, our best friend is often the one we think of last, if at all."

Was she talking about Stephen? Was she sorry she hadn't thought of him as a possible husband? Then why had she turned him down flat when he'd proposed?

"I don't know," Susanna said into the silence. "There were so few *Youngie* in the Ventana that I didn't have best friends who were boys. I was just glad there were enough other girls my age to make a very small buddy bunch."

Lena smiled. "I suppose they're going crazy for him here. He's a nice-looking man."

Somehow it felt dishonest, talking about Stephen behind his back. "We haven't seen much of him here in town." Well, that was the truth. "We've just had a hundred-year storm and all the hands are up on the allotments looking for calves."

"I heard about that. Eight feet of snow, it said on the news."

Susanna nodded. "A lot of people were stranded on the highway and taking refuge with strangers. Here at the Inn, we had six anglers who couldn't leave, plus my family. It was quite a houseful."

"I guess my timing is *gut*, then. Nothing but sunshine and warm weather forecasted for this week."

"I hope it keeps up. We're to host a barn raising this Tuesday, and the foundation needs to be completely cured by then."

And hopefully Lena would have concluded her visit and gone home.

"So you think Stephen is up looking for calves?"

"I expect so. He's the foreman, so he'd be responsible for counting heads and making sure none of them got lost."

"Can a person drive up there?"

Susanna tried to imagine driving up on BLM land with that little car outside. "There aren't many roads—and what's up there are just cut lines from the old logging outfits. You'd do better on a horse."

"I don't ride. It was against the *Ordnung* at home, and goodness knows that was all that mattered in our house."

Susanna wasn't certain her bitter tone required a response. "You might do better to ask at the Bar K. They'll have heard from him, and know more about how the search is going."

Lena eyed her. "He was your foreman. You must have known him pretty well. Doesn't he keep in touch with you?"

Susanna lifted a shoulder, doing her best to seem casual. "We'll see him at church on Sunday. We're in the same district."

"Hm. Maybe I should go."

"If you stay with the Keims, you could go with them."

"No, I'll be here."

"Only until Friday morning. Remember? We have guests coming in that afternoon who have booked that room."

Lena gazed at her as though Susanna were simple. "Surely you can book them into another one."

Trying not to show how surprised she was, Susanna said, "They're all reserved. Summer is our busy season, and all the storm cancellations are trying to re-book."

"Hm." The baby yawned, and Lena glanced down at the carrier.

Time to change the subject. "What's the *Boppli*'s name?"

"Curtis. Curt for short."

"After his father?"

"No," Lena said in English. "Why would you say that?"

Susanna switched languages, too. "My brother is named after Dat—Marlon Tobias. We call him Tobias, though."

"Well, we're not Amish." Lena rose. "If you give me directions, I'll run over to the Keim place and see about Stephen. Okay if I leave Curtis here?"

Susanna was so shocked it was a few seconds before she could speak. "Leave a baby this young with someone he doesn't know?"

"Sure. You're Amish. Probably handled a hundred kids. There's a bottle of pumped milk ready to go in the baby bag. I'll leave it for you if he gets hungry."

"Lena, I have work to do. We have guests com—"

"And I'm a guest. I'll give you my credit card when I get back. If I can arrange it with the Keim family, I'll stay for—" She paused. "I'll stay there."

"You'll come back soon?"

Lena grinned at her. "What's the matter, no practice with babies? Don't worry, I'll only be an hour. Directions?"

Dismayed, Susanna drew a map on the back of an envelope, and in five minutes she was alone with a stranger's baby and his bag of supplies. When Mamm and Luke came in half an hour later, the bathrooms had not yet received their clean towels, and Susanna was still sitting at the table with the plate of cookies, two empty glasses, and the baby carrier.

Mamm looked around for evidence of company. "Is Sara here?"

"This isn't Nathan," Susanna said in a voice that didn't

quite sound like her own. "This is Curtis Johnson, from Monte Vista, Colorado, who is younger."

The little boy blinked up at Mamm's astonished face and his own crumpled. Small as he was, he let out quite a roar. Without hesitation, Mamm scooped him out of the carrier and cocked an eyebrow at the bag. Susanna fished around in it, located the bottle, and handed it to her.

But Curtis didn't want the bottle. He wanted his mother, not to be abandoned in a house full of strangers. He turned his face away and fat tears rolled down his little cheeks.

"I have a few words to say, but since they aren't fit for the ears of *Gott*'s children, I will keep them to myself," Mamm said over the wails. "Whose child is this?"

"Her name is Lena Schrock Johnson. Apparently she's staying with us tonight. After she gets back from tracking down Stephen."

"Stephen Kurtz?" Mamm offered the bottle again, but Curtis just increased the volume. "Our Stephen?"

Under normal circumstances, Susanna would have hugged that little slip of the tongue to herself and delighted in it. But these circumstances were far from normal. He was no more theirs than he was Lena's. "He told me she was married. And maybe she is, but she's not wearing a ring like the *Englisch* usually do."

"Here, *Liewi*." They were the first words Luke had spoken since he'd come in behind Mamm. He reached out. "Give him to me."

He cuddled the bawling bundle and began to walk slow circles around the dining table. The volume decreased just a little, and on the next circuit, Mamm handed him the bottle. When the baby accepted it, Susanna felt the tension in her shoulders loosen a little.

"For two cents I'd tell her to go stay at the motel by the neurology clinic," Mamm said in a tone that told Susanna she'd take one cent. "Or the Rocking Diamond."

"Nobody can afford the Rocking Diamond," Susanna reminded her as her sense of humor trickled back.

"I'd omit that little fact. What kind of a woman leaves her *Boppli* with strangers and just drives away?"

"The kind who wants to talk to a man without her wedding ring or her child," Susanna said. *The kind who wants to appear single.*

"Maybe we should warn him," Luke said in a quiet, soothing voice. Curtis ignored him, completely focused on the bottle.

"It's probably already too late." Susanna dragged herself out of the chair, feeling as though she had weights tied to every extremity. "While Curtis is busy, I'd better get the towels into the bathrooms. And make sure our unexpected guest has everything she needs."

Except Stephen. Please, mei Vater, surely she can't have come to tell Stephen she's changed her mind.

The Bar K Ranch

Stephen stepped out of the shower in the bunkhouse, having washed away a long day's mud and calf spatter. Though all thirty-eight calves were accounted for, he and Josiah and the hands had still ridden up on the allotment today, just to make certain that all was well and the animals were all able to find grazing, thus gaining back any weight they'd lost during the storm.

As he dried off and dressed, Mark Steiner called up from below. "Stephen! You have company!"

Susanna. He hadn't seen her in several days, and the thought that she might have felt it, too, and manufactured an errand to come and see him, warmed his heart to a glow. He called down the stairwell, "Be right there."

He took two extra seconds to run a comb through his damp hair and to ram his stocking feet into his good pair of boots. Then he loped downstairs and out the side door into the late afternoon sun.

An *Englisch* car was parked in the yard. Probably someone to see Josiah. Had Susanna borrowed one of the Yoder buggies, or had she caught a ride over here? Maybe Tobias had had a delivery again, and—

"Stephen."

The voice was familiar, but since he was looking for Susanna, it didn't really register. Not until an *Englisch* woman wearing jeans and a T-shirt stepped out of the car and walked toward him did his brain catch up with the evidence of his own eyes.

"What's the matter?" Lena Schrock said in English with a smile. "I'm not a ghost."

It took a second for his mouth to work—a second in which he realized that not only had two of the hands found something unnecessary to do in the yard, Sylvia Keim was over in the vegetable garden, thirty feet away. All three were well within earshot.

"What are you doing here?" finally came out, sounding winded. Well, he felt winded. As though someone had given him a hard push to make him do something he didn't want to do.

"Visiting you." She smiled at him, the old smile full of mischief, her big blue eyes twinkling and her blond hair cut short, swinging around her jawline as she shook it back.

He glanced into the car, which contained her handbag on the passenger seat and a small suitcase in the back. "Are you here with your husband?" For a moment, he couldn't recall the man's name. Then it came to him. "Eric? And the baby?"

"No. I just got here. It's quite a drive from the Wet Valley."

"Two days at least," he agreed, feeling a little adrift and wondering why he was making small talk. "A lot farther than when I went down from Chama with the horse trailer." He gestured toward the house and its welcoming veranda. "Can I offer you something? Are you hungry?"

"No, I got a burger in town."

"Do you have someplace to stay?" She couldn't stay in the bunkhouse with a bunch of guys. But with Sharon and Bethany here, how many empty beds remained in the big house? Maybe he should go in and ask.

"I booked into that Amish Inn. And who should I meet but the folks you used to work for. The daughter was really nice. Gave me some cookies and a map to find this place." She gazed around at the paddocks and finally in the direction of the garden, where the steady *chunk* of a hoe told him Sylvia was loosening the soil the snowmelt had packed down. The hands had found something else to do in the barn.

And all the while, Stephen's mind reeled at the image in his head of Susanna opening the door to discover Lena Schrock, of all people, on her front porch asking for a room.

What must she be thinking right now?

Probably a lot more than he was capable of at the moment. For the life of him, he could not figure out why Lena was here, alone, and without the child she would have had only a few months ago. A hundred questions flapped around in his head like a flock of starlings, but not one of them landed long enough to make sense.

Her gaze snapped back to him. "Look, Stephen, we need to talk, but not right now. I'm so exhausted I can barely see straight. I just wanted to let you know I was in town. How soon can we get together?"

Tomorrow was Thursday. "I have to take a saddle over to Joshua Miller tomorrow. I tried to do it last week, but we had a storm—"

"I know. I saw it on the news. Well, how far do you have to go? Can I come with you?"

"I'll ask Josiah if I can borrow a buggy." It would offer as much privacy as Stephen could expect on short notice. "I can pick you up at the Inn at nine."

"No. Not the Inn. I'll come and get you here, in the car."

"I'd like to say hello to the Millers," he protested. "See how they're recovering from the storm."

"They're doing just fine. All booked up for the weekend. Just humor me, will you? This is important, but if I start talking about it now, I'll go all to pieces." She turned away, her head bowed, and put a hand on the car door. "Tomorrow at nine. The saddle ought to fit in the backseat all right."

He shrugged. "Sure. Fine. Are you sure you don't want to—"

"Nice to see you, Stephen." She flashed him a wobbly smile and got in.

He had a sinking feeling that whatever she needed to talk about couldn't be good. He could understand her husband not coming with her on a road trip if he had a job, but the absence of the baby and her reluctance to talk about him was not only puzzling, it was ominous.

He'd never seen Lena drive before. She backed the car around with every appearance of confidence, and when she was pointed into the lane, gave it the gas. The rear wheels spun in a mud puddle until the front ones got a grip on firmer ground. With a wave, she took off down the lane as though it never occurred to her there could be a neighbor coming in a buggy or chickens pecking in the way or anything.

Mark ambled out of the barn door and cocked an eyebrow at him. "I'm sure she didn't do that on purpose."

Stephen gazed at the rooster-tail of mud and dirty water dripping down his front, covering his clean shirt and pants from chest to boots. "I'm sure she didn't. But she hasn't had her license all that long."

"Who was she?"

"An old family friend."

"Your family has *Englisch* friends who visit for five minutes, cover you in mud, and leave without saying sorry?"

"*Ja*, I suppose we do." With a sigh, Stephen turned for the door, and the second shower and change of clothes that afternoon.

❧ 18 ❧

THE BAR K RANCH

Thursday morning, June 9

THE KEIM FAMILY'S curiosity about Lena's visit yesterday had been so great that Stephen had to give them some kind of explanation. He continued to pass it off as a visit from an old friend from Colorado—which was true—and omitted the part about her being under the *Bann*. All they knew was that she had chosen the world over the Amish way of life, and that she was on her way to somewhere else. She'd kindly offered to take him and the saddle over to Millers', which was both convenient for him and the act of an old friend.

If Josiah and Kathryn thought any different, they didn't say a word to him. They probably had plenty to say to each other in private, though.

Just to be on the safe side, Stephen wore an old shirt and pants, and his comfortable old pair of work boots. If she was going to spray him with mud again, at least he would be prepared.

When she arrived promptly at nine, he loaded the saddle

into the backseat of her car, noting that the suitcase was gone. He settled into the passenger seat and fastened the seatbelt, then put the paper sack he carried on the floor between his feet.

"What's that?" She started the engine, fastened her own seatbelt, and rolled out a little more slowly than she had yesterday. The chickens, he noticed, got out of her way and took refuge under the shrubbery next to the house.

"Kathryn sent a snack along in case we got hungry. Two hand pies and a couple of pieces of cake."

Lena laughed. "How long does she think this is going to take?"

With a lift of one shoulder, he said, "The saddle? Probably not long. The visit might be longer. Turn right here, and then left on Glacier Road about three miles down."

"Visit." She made the turn and accelerated. "I haven't heard that expression for a long time. Well, we'll drop off your saddle and then find someplace quiet to talk and eat our cake. I haven't had cake in ages."

He didn't seem to have much choice in their itinerary. If it was the kind of visit that meant tears, he'd just as soon it happened well away from Joshua and Sara's place.

"The harness maker's name is Joshua Miller," he said as they flew down the road. She sure drove fast—as though making up for lost time during all those buggy years. "His dad Reuben is the brother of Rachel's late husband, Marlon. So Josh and Susanna are cousins."

"That's convenient. Is that why Rachel moved back here?"

"It's nice to go where you have family," he said mildly. "Rachel grew up here."

"Is that why you moved here, too? To be with a family you knew?"

He shook his head. "I moved here because Josiah offered me the foreman's job. I didn't know the Millers were here until I arrived."

"Yikes. Amish grapevine fail. That doesn't happen very often."

"Maybe not. I was just glad to get the work. I like Josiah as a boss, and you can't beat the Keim kitchen."

"Do you see Rachel and her family much? Wait—is this the turn?"

"Yep, left here. I see them at church. And Susanna and I and an *Englisch* mother and her little boy were all snowed in at Joshua's place during the blizzard."

"That must have been fun. Not."

How *Englisch* she sounded. He could still hear the *Deitsch* cadence in her speech, though. She probably wasn't even aware of it enough to try to iron it out.

"It was pretty scary. If the *Englisch* woman hadn't seen the light, I'm not sure she and her boy would have survived. Their car was completely buried in snow and invisible. Like lots of others."

"Guess I picked the right week to come, then."

"You could say that. Here's Dutchman Road. Make a right and two miles down you'll see the sign on the right—Miller Saddle and Harness."

This time Joshua was home and waiting for him with a smile of greeting. With the saddle safely in the shop, the two men concluded their business, and Stephen declined the invitation to come in for *Kaffee*, much as he wanted to. It was one thing for him to disobey the *Bann* and keep company with Lena. But he wasn't about to put that on anyone else, particularly since he was deliberately not telling any of his Amish neighbors Lena's status in the church. To them, she was now

ADINA SENFT

simply an *Englisch* woman, and did not touch their lives in any way.

But she was touching his. And now was the time for him to find out why.

"There's a scenic overlook up there." In the car heading west once more, he pointed to a sign for the county park. "Kathryn says it's a good place for a picnic."

She made the turn, and a few minutes later they arrived at the overlook, which was also the parking lot for a trailhead. A single pickup was parked at the far end. At this end, a couple of big flat rocks made a good place to sit with their feet swinging, the trail winding down below their feet to the river in the distance. They could look out over half the valley, including the Miller hay farm.

He'd brought along the sack of food, but she didn't seem inclined to investigate the contents. Maybe the breakfast at the Wild Rose Amish Inn had been enough to carry a person through to lunch. The breeze tugged at his straw summer hat, and he screwed it down a little. He didn't much want to go running off down the slope after it, especially with a ten-foot drop just below. At the base of the rocks on which they sat, clumps of blue and purple lupine bloomed, mixed with wild sweet peas, pink and white.

He spent a lot of time outdoors, but not so much just sitting still and absorbing the beauty of *Gott*'s creation. He was more used to searching out the brown and black hides of cattle in the trees than the delicate shades of wildflowers. Had Susanna ever been up here? Today would be a *gut* day for a hike down to the river—just to look at it. Not to chase a hat. And then maybe he might pick some flowers for her and—

"So aren't you going to ask me?"

Stephen came back to himself and his company. "I figured you had a story to tell, and you'd get to it in your own time."

"It isn't a story, Stephen. It's the truth."

"Just a figure of speech."

"Somehow it feels like you're not all that happy to see me."

"Of course I am. It's just strange, is all. I don't understand why the baby isn't with you."

"You don't think Eric can care for his own child?"

"From what I remember, it isn't his child."

With a huff, Lena settled herself more comfortably on the rock. "Fine, Grossmammi. Curtis is at the Inn. Susanna and Rachel are looking after him for an hour."

A tingle of shock ran through him. She'd left the baby with them yesterday, too, then. With an inn to run, and their own business to attend to. No matter how much they loved children, how might they have felt about that? "Too bad. I'd have liked to meet him."

Now she turned to him, almost eagerly. "Would you? Do you want to see him?"

"Well, sure. You went through a lot to have him. Is he a *gut Boppli*?" He switched to *Deitsch*, the language of home and family.

"*Ja*, he's the best." She switched, too. "Always hungry, though. I have to keep a bottle handy all the time. But Stephen, I didn't drive all the way up here to look at the scenery and talk about bottle feeding."

"I didn't suppose so."

"When you came—last fall. You came all that way to ask me a question."

"I did. And you gave me an answer."

"I know. I was a fool. I turned down the man who really loved me for a man who only thought he did. And now—"

"Lena, I didn't—"

"Please. Let me get all this out. Me and Eric, well, we had a fight a couple of days ago. And I bet you can guess what it was about."

Was she kidding? "I have no idea. I haven't seen you since last autumn."

"*You*, Stephen." Her eyes pleaded with him. "We fought over *you*. Because Eric never believed that I married him for love."

"I'm sorry to hear that." It was the truth. There wasn't much else he could say.

"The thing is, I did. That's the tragedy. I'm afraid I lost my temper and said some things I couldn't take back, which only made it worse. He told me to go to you, if that was what I wanted, and I said that was what *he* wanted, not me, and he threw a bunch of my things out on the lawn with a suitcase and some money. So I packed up Curtis and came. Just to make him sorry."

With a growing sense of horror that two people could be so hammer-headed with each other, Stephen worked through this scene in his mind. "And now that you've done that, are you going back?"

"Well, it's clear that he doesn't love me."

"I wouldn't say that." All he could see were the actions of a man who had been badly hurt.

She sighed, and he was pretty sure she rolled her eyes. "Stephen, you've never been married." When he didn't reply to the obvious, she went on, "Sometimes two people just can't work out their differences."

"Not from two states away."

"But the thing is, you've always been there for me."

"So has Eric. After Curtis's father rode off into the sunset, Eric was there. He made a home for you."

"He let me move into his crappy little house."

"His home," he repeated. "He put a ring on your finger. Which seems to be missing."

She drew back. "Ouch."

"What did you do, throw it in the lake in another fit of temper?"

"Stephen Kurtz, when did you get so mean?"

"I'm not being mean," he said mildly. "I'm asking a reasonable question."

"It's in my suitcase." She swung around to face the view again, a pleat of irritation between her brows. Then she took a deep breath. "Like I said, you've always been there for me. In those years when my parents put the *Ordnung* ahead of their children."

Most Amish parents did, and that was how their children learned to put *Gott*'s will first. But saying so would only make her angry. She had had the most difficult time subjecting her own will to both her heavenly Father and her earthly one.

"And later, when I got pregnant, all I had to do was tell you, and you dropped everything to come and help. I realize now that I was staring love in the face all that time, and never saw it."

"There are different kinds of love." He didn't like the sound of this. "I came the way a brother comes to help his sister."

"A brother doesn't *propose* to his sister." Now she turned to him. "You love me. I know you do. Stephen, if I get a divorce, we can be together. You'd make a far better father to Curtis than Eric ever will, and—" She stopped, squinting up at him in the bright sunshine. "What's the matter?"

He didn't even remember scrambling to his feet at the word *divorce*, but here he was, standing. She got up, too. And moved closer, slipping her arms around him and leaning into him for a hug.

He would rather be hugged by a bear. At least bears were predictable.

As gently as he could, he turned her and led her away from the long drop below the stones to the level gravel of the parking lot, close to her car. Then he released her. "Lena, I've learned since that day what love really means. What you saw in Colorado last fall was the action of a romantic boy, thoughtless and impulsive, and compelled by old loyalties. Since then, I've grown up in my head and my heart. And my heart belongs to someone else. It always has."

Her mouth dropped open. "Who?" Her eyes lost their focus, as though she were thumbing through memories the way some people shuffled cards. Then she pinned him with that wide blue gaze. "It's her, isn't it? Susanna. You told me you'd left a home behind to come to me. I thought you meant the ranch. But you meant a future home. With her." When he didn't reply, she pressed. "Didn't you?"

"I did mean the ranch. Susanna was part of it. And yes, I left the possibility of a home of my own behind. I knew that. But I was too foolish, too caught up in being the hero who would rescue you, to count the cost. I know now that losing her again is a price I'm not willing to pay."

"Does she feel the same way?"

She was far too calm. Friendly, almost. The old Lena. But he didn't dare hope she'd abandoned her crazy idea.

"I don't know. We're still *gut* friends. But I'm going to court her again. I believe that *Gott* has led us both here to the Siksika to bring us together, this time inside His will."

An expression of distaste crossed her pretty face like a catspaw of wind on a pond, there and then gone. "So that's a no, then. It's God's will that you happened to move here at the same time, so you're going to abandon a girl who loves you and chase a girl who only wants to be friends."

"I'm going to obey *Gott's wille*. And you should honor the vows you made to Eric and go back to him. Put your wedding ring on and tell him what happened here. Let him be a father. Talk to him. Running away never solves anything—it just makes things worse."

She stared at him incredulously. "What gives you the right to tell me what to do?"

"Nothing at all. But you know what you need to do to make things right again. I don't have to tell you."

"Oooh, you are just so—so *Amish!* Fine. Go ahead and take back what you said when you proposed."

"A proposal you refused."

"There is no use talking to you if you keep throwing my sins in my face. I'm done here. Good-bye, Stephen. Have a nice life." She wrenched open the car door and got in. "And maybe once in a while you can think of what you've done to mine."

She started the car, backed out into the lot, spun the wheel and hit the gas.

This time he had the presence of mind to step out of the way of the flying gravel from the rear tires. The sound of the engine faded away into the trees, and in a moment he saw the car below on the road, flashing between the pines.

Knowing Lena, it wasn't likely she'd change her mind and come back to take him home.

He ambled over to the little paper sack of food abandoned on the rocks. Picked it up and felt the warmth of the sun on his shoulders. Above him, a hawk balanced lazily on the updraft, and below, a ground squirrel peeked above the rocks as though wondering whether it was safe to come out.

Stephen fished a hand pie out of the sack and bit into it. Straight from the Keim kitchen—rich and savory and full of flavor. Still warm, too. He walked over to the trail head and started down the trail that would bring him out near the bridge over the Siksika River. He would have to thank Kathryn for pressing the food on him as they left. Without it, he'd have been pretty hungry by the time he got to the Circle M, where he could hitch a ride into town.

Because the only place he wanted to be right now was at the Wild Rose Amish Inn, looking into Susanna's eyes as he told her everything in his heart.

❧ 19 ❧

THE WILD ROSE AMISH INN

"OH, THANK GOODNESS." Little Curtis was screaming on Susanna's shoulder, his limbs rigid with outrage, fat tears rolling down his scarlet cheeks. "Mamm is coming. See? She's just outside, parking the car."

It was all she could do not to push the child into Lena's arms when she came in the door. Instead, she stayed in the window seat in the sitting room, holding the baby, the relieved greeting dying on her lips at the jerky movements and danger flags of color in their guest's face.

"Did you have a nice visit at Joshua and Sara's?" she ventured. "Look, Curtis, here's Mamm. See her?"

"He doesn't understand *Deitsch*," Lena said impatiently. "He's only six months old."

"It's not me he wants, no matter what language I speak," Susanna said. She got up. "If you take him, he'll likely quiet down."

"Did you feed him?"

No, I've let him scream with hunger all this time. "*Ja*, he took the whole bottle. He's in a fresh diaper. He just wants his *Mamm*."

With a huff of breath, Lena dropped her purse on the one of the stairs and took the baby. She sat in the armchair in the L-shaped nook made by the bookcases. What blessed relief when his screams became crying, and then snuffling, and then hiccups against his mother's shoulder.

"Poor *Boppli*," Susanna said, producing a tissue so Lena could wipe his nose and face. "He's a little young to be left with strangers yet, I think."

"And you say this out of your vast experience?" The tone matched the high color in her cheeks.

Susanna declined to meet fire with fire. "I got plenty of experience with Gracie and Benny. It wasn't so long ago when Lily Anne and I would each have a baby in our arms, and it was anybody's guess which one would scream for Mamm when it was their turn for me to hold them."

"Not very good with kids, then."

Something must have happened. Why else would Lena be so irritable and unkind?

"Is everything all right?" she asked cautiously. Upstairs, she could hear Mamm humming "Just a Closer Walk With Thee" as she arranged flowers in the vases of each room before the weekend guests arrived tomorrow. The twins were outside with the baby chicks, who were sleek adolescents now, and full of curiosity about the world. It wasn't exactly private here, but no one could sit silent and just let a woman fume without trying to do something. It was bad for the baby.

With a deep breath, Lena seemed to realize how she sounded, and she relaxed. Maybe it was the soothing weight of her son. Or maybe Susanna had managed to strike the right note with her at last.

Susanna slid into the window seat, her feet tucked up under her skirts. "I don't mean to pry into your business, but did you see Stephen?"

"Oh, yes. We took the saddle over to Joshua and Sara's, and then we went up to the overlook for a picnic."

Susanna blinked. "Oh," was all she could think of to say. No wonder she'd taken all this time, if they'd enjoyed their picnic and then she had to drive from one side of the valley to the other to take Stephen home afterward.

"We had some things to talk about," Lena explained. "And ground squirrels don't gossip."

"Only among themselves," Susanna joked.

Lena didn't seem to find this amusing. She didn't even seem to hear. "I was so happy that we got some things resolved. The most important being—" Her face softened, and she smiled, not at Susanna, but the way a woman smiles when she thinks of someone important to her.

A flare of alarm flickered through Susanna's stomach.

"He still loves me, Susanna." With a happy sigh, she cuddled the baby. "After all this time, after all I've done, he loves me."

She couldn't have moved if she tried. Susanna's entire being was frozen into ice, her eyes wide and staring as her worst fear —the one that had kept her awake last night into the small hours—came true right in front of her.

"I don't know how we're going to manage it. But to begin, I'm leaving now—as soon as I can pack—to go back to Colorado. I'll tell Eric the truth, and maybe it will mean divorce, but lots of people divorce and marry again."

The word *divorce* flashed like fire along every vein in Susanna's body, and released her from the paralysis of shock. "Marry again?"

"Yes. We'll finally be the family we were always meant to be. I'm sure you know that my family always expected it."

"Y-yes, but—"

Lena hid her face in the crook of the baby's neck. "I know I've made some mistakes, but he's willing to help me put them right."

"But—but that would mean—"

"We'd both live an *Englisch* life. I know."

"And he wants this?" Susanna's voice came out as a whisper, devoid of actual sound.

"He told me to go as soon as I could. Getting things straight with Eric can't come soon enough." Her eyes became dreamy, looking into the future. "And then Curtis will have a real father, who loves him and who will show him how to be a good man. Won't you, punkin?" She nuzzled the baby's face.

The poor child had exhausted himself and was sound asleep. Susanna almost wished he would wake up and scream. And cry. Because Susanna felt as though she were falling through the air, and it would demonstrate perfectly what she felt. Or would feel, as soon as she landed with a crash.

"I thought you should know, before I left. A lot earlier than I expected!" Lena rose, the baby on her shoulder. "My credit card is in the wallet in my purse, if you don't mind checking me out? I'll just run upstairs and put Curtis in the car seat. It won't take long to pack up. Not more than five minutes."

What a hurry she was in to start her new life. To jettison one man and reunite with another.

But Stephen—to leave Susanna again—and even worse, leave the church—leave *Gott* Himself for the sake of a divorced woman—

It was unthinkable. And yet, here was Lena, joyfully ready to go and do everything he said.

It's not true, whispered a voice in the back of her mind. *It can't be true.*

And yet, how could it not be? He'd done it before. He'd left for this same woman, planning never to return. Was he making arrangements even now for a horse trailer and driver?

How could this be happening?

What was wrong with her that she was never good enough? Only second best. Only ever a friend, never a wife.

Upstairs, Lena dropped something. Susanna jerked as though she'd been struck.

Like a marionette, she pulled herself to her feet. Hunted in Lena's purse for the wallet containing the credit card. Ran it through the card reader that attached to the Inn's phone. Checked her out.

When Lena came downstairs and asked if Susanna could bring the suitcase down while she buckled in the car seat, Susanna obeyed, and brought her purse along, too, the receipt for one night inside it. Then stood there like a post while Lena backed around and drove out of the empty parking lot, splashing through the last of the puddles from the melted snow.

The sound of the engine slowed at the intersection, then faded rapidly away as it headed east toward the highway that would take her south to the interstate.

Mamm came down the stairs and joined her on the porch stairs. "Was that Lena? Did she come back from Keims'?"

"She's gone."

"I see that. I'm glad she took her *Boppli* this time. Where's she gone now?"

"Back to Colorado."

Mamm made a noise in her throat. "Didn't get what she wanted?"

Susanna swallowed. "Oh, *ja*. She got what she wanted. Everything and more."

Then she turned and went into the house.

"Susanna...?"

She walked into her room. Closed the door. And for the first time since they'd moved in, she turned the lock.

Uncomprehending, Rachel stood motionless on the porch, staring through the open door at the empty hallway down which her daughter had disappeared. Then she collected herself and closed it before the flies got in. Hardly aware of what she was doing, she sank onto the wrought-iron bench next to it the guests used to take off their wet fly-fishing boots.

Never in all her life had she seen such a white, frozen look of utter despair on her daughter's face. Not even when Stephen had left the first time. Because then, Susanna had still clung to the hope that he would be back. That while something terrible had happened, he would deal with it, and in a couple of weeks he would roll back into the yard with the horse trailer and they would pick up where they had left off. Months of silence had gone by before Susanna had finally brought herself to let go of that hope. It had meant tears and rage from a person whose emotions were close to the surface, but she had worked through them before she'd resigned herself to his never coming back.

What she had been through since that day she'd seen him ride past with the Eicher turnout, Rachel could only guess. Her girl had ridden the highs of seeing him again—of coming to some sort of understanding during the blizzard—of daring to allow a tiny flame of hope in the face of all odds. And now this?

The lack of expression on her white face had frightened Rachel. It was the face of a woman who had been struck a death blow and just hadn't fallen yet.

The rapid clip-clop of a horse and buggy penetrated her consciousness only when she heard the hollow thump of hooves on the bridge into their empty parking lot. Malena Miller pulled up next to the porch and Stephen got out on the passenger side.

"I brought you a delivery," she said cheerfully. "I had to take a quilt to Rose, and met Stephen at the bottom of our lane looking for a ride."

This made absolutely no sense to Rachel. "What was he doing there?" she asked blankly. Hadn't he gone back to Keims'?

"*Denki* for the lift, Malena," he said, thanking Hester with a pat on the nose as he came around the front.

"Anytime. I'll see you at church Sunday—I'll be coming to this side with Alden."

"See you then."

"Bye, Rachel. I have another stop to make." Her grin as she guided the horse around and headed out of the parking lot told Rachel that might just include a visit to the blacksmith's shop on the far side of Yoder's Variety Store.

"Is Susanna home?" Hope and anticipation shone in his eyes, and Rachel's confusion only increased.

"*Ja*, but I'm not sure now is a *gut* time to see her."

He stopped in his beeline for the door, and Rachel seized the moment to take his arm, leading him around to the patio off the kitchen, where they couldn't be heard from the family wing. The chickens were in the dust bath, the twins nowhere to be seen. She sat at the little garden table and after a moment of hesitation, he sat opposite.

"Stephen, what is going on?" she demanded without preamble. "All I know are two things—Lena Schrock has gone back to Colorado, and my daughter's face looks like death."

Alarm widened his eyes. "Is she sick?"

"Not physically. But inside, in her heart, something terrible has happened."

He half rose. "I have to talk to her."

"Not just yet. Tell me why my daughter thinks Lena got *everything she wanted*—" She made air quotes with her fingers. "—and yet, you somehow wound up all the way over at the Circle M looking for a ride to town."

He took off his hat and raked his fingers through his hair, then put it back on. "Lena said she wanted to talk. So she offered to drive me and the saddle over to Joshua's, and after I dropped it off, we went up to the overlook."

"And what does a married woman with a baby have to talk about with a single man?"

He couldn't look her in the face. Instead, he looked almost ashamed at having to answer. "She had a big fight with her husband, and wants to get a divorce. She drove all the way up here hoping I'd come to the rescue. Again."

She got what she wanted. Everything and more.

The wind brushed the nape of her neck and Rachel shivered. "And did you?"

"*Neh*. I told her what was right, not what she wanted to hear. I said I was going to court Susanna, because I believe *Gott* brought both of us here to this valley to be together. I told Lena she should put her wedding ring on, go back to her husband, and make it right with him."

"What did she want to hear? What did she expect you would do?"

"Marry her, I guess. She would divorce Eric, and I would leave the church, and we'd all live happily ever after under the *Bann*."

"She must be crazy," came out of Rachel's mouth before she could stop it.

"She doesn't think things through," he said, shaking his head. "But I want no part of it."

"So then what?"

The corner of his mouth lifted in what might pass for a smile. "She drove away and left me there. Came straight here to get the baby and her things, I guess."

"She left you up there on the overlook?" Rachel supposed it was lucky they hadn't gone to Libby for their little talk. She began to wish she'd eavesdropped on that girl's conversation with Susanna, because something was very wrong. "So you walked to the Circle M. And came here instead of going home."

He nodded. "The only thing I want in the world is to talk to your daughter. Will you let me do that now?"

Rachel wasted no more time. "I'll tell you something. Those two had a conversation, and I don't think it bore any resemblance to the one you and I have just had. You can try, but she's in her room, and she may not come out."

He straightened, and the shame fell away like the snow off the boughs of a pine. "Then I'll camp in front of her door until she does. Or go in through the window. But I have to talk to her."

"Stay away from me." A voice Rachel hardly recognized came from behind them, and she turned. Susanna stood on the neat bricks of the patio as though at the side of an open grave.

"I heard your voices. Whatever you have to say to me, Stephen, I don't want to hear it. If you don't go to Colorado, then I'll be the one to leave. Because this is the last time I ever want to see your face."

20

SUSANNA HAD NOT KNOWN a human heart could contain this much pain. And somehow, saying such harsh words to Stephen made it even worse. But she had to cut him out of her life. Use the sharp edge of her tongue to make the separation clean and permanent. Otherwise, she would never, ever heal. She would carry this wound around with her forever, and her whole soul shuddered away from the prospect.

Mamm rose and, without a word, went inside through the kitchen door.

Nobody else seemed inclined to leave, so Susanna turned to do what she'd said.

"Susanna," Stephen said hoarsely. "Don't go. Talk to me."

"There is nothing left to say. You've made your choice. I've made mine. That's that."

"*Ja*, I've made my choice, for sure and certain. I choose *you*."

Did he really think that she didn't know what had passed between him and Lena up there on that overlook? "Lying is a sin." She turned her back on him and took two steps away, and the next thing she knew, he had spun her around and taken her in his arms.

The nerve! She got both hands between them, against his chest, and pushed with all of her might.

It did not one bit of good. Stephen had too much practice in wrestling calves and swinging a lariat. All right, then, she'd do the opposite. She let her fists slide to her sides and stood there, inert, lifeless, waiting for him to let her go.

But he didn't. With infinite tenderness, he gathered her closer, so that her cheek fell against his shoulder, and her nose found that special place under his jaw. He smelled of dust and sweat and clean cotton—just like always.

Oh, this just wasn't fair.

"I vow to you here and now," he said, his voice rumbling against her chest, "that there is only one woman for me, and her name is Susanna Miller. Whatever Lena told you isn't true. Did you hear what I said to your *mamm*?"

Susanna shook her head before she remembered she was supposed to be inert.

"I told Lena to put on her wedding ring, go home to her husband, and do what was right. I bet she didn't tell you that part."

Being inert stopped working. Susanna looked up into his eyes and the love there brought a lump into her throat. But she had to fight her way through to the truth. "She said you loved her."

"I never told her so. Not even the first time, when I proposed. I was still grieving the loss of you, even though I'd done it to myself."

"Then why would she say such a thing?" Her voice cracked. "Tell such a lie to me?"

"Did she actually use my name? Did she say, 'Stephen loves me'?"

Every word was branded on Susanna's memory, still burning around the edges. "*Neh*, she only said *he*. But she meant you, I'm sure of ..." Her voice faded as memory flooded in. Lena had never used Stephen's name. She'd used her husband's, though—Eric. But—but— "She said that getting things resolved with Eric couldn't come soon enough. She said that Curtis would have a father who loves him, who would show him how to be a good man. She meant you. After she got a divorce. That was what she'd get straight."

"It would be just like Lena to make you think she was talking about me, and all the while be talking about Eric. So technically she wouldn't be lying."

"But *divorce?*"

"Why not throw that in to shock you? It shocked me when she said it. She really expected me to walk away from you a second time. As I told your mother, in Lena's mind she had it all planned out. She'd divorce her husband, I would leave the church, and we'd all live happily ever after. What's a little thing like *die Meinding* to get in the way?"

Susanna exhaled a short puff of air. What kind of woman would drive for two days to ask a baptized Amish man to do such a crazy thing?

He squeezed her tightly, and then released her. When her wobbly knees made her turn to find the nearest chair, she saw that two glasses of lemonade and a plate of fresh strawberries had magically appeared on the little round outdoor table.

Mamm. Who clearly trusted that all would come out right.

"*Kumm mit, Liewi.*" Stephen took her hand and led her over, but instead of sitting across from her, he hooked the chair he'd been sitting in with one hand and drew it up beside her, close enough to take her hand. "Do you believe me?" he asked softly.

She took a sip of lemonade to moisten her dry mouth. "It's hard to believe that a woman could be so wicked. Could deliberately hurt another woman right down to the heart."

"I saw her face change when I told her my heart belonged to someone else. She guessed right away that it was you. Maybe that's why she took off without me. She wanted to do as much damage as she could and get out of town before anyone could call her to account for it."

Susanna shook her head in wonder. "That poor woman. To have to live with that knowledge inside herself—that she was capable of such a thing."

"I'm just glad neither of us has to live with it. I hope we never hear from her again. And that once she's done the right thing by her husband and son, she'll find peace in the end."

"I hope so." Susanna lifted her lashes. "Your heart belongs to me? Really?"

Oh, that smile that came so rarely, and was so *wunderbaar* when it did! "It has since the day you roped me in the home paddock at the Four Winds. Remember?"

Now it was her turn to smile, just a tiny bit gleeful. "Do I ever. Oh, I was so mad at you. Teasing me until I couldn't stand it, and then thinking you could get away with it. Guess I showed you, *nix?*"

"I guess you did. Any woman who can rope a man while he's running as fast as his boots can carry him is a woman I want on my side no matter what."

She laughed—she'd stood by him, all right, reeling him in like a fish until he stood in front of her with that rope tight around him while she gave him a piece of her mind.

The laughter faded to a smile, and she confessed softly,

"That was a *gut* day. You kissed me that evening. And from that day, my heart belonged to you, too." Her lashes flicked up. "Even as the months wore on, and I gave up hope that you'd come back. It was terrible for me when we moved off the Four Winds—what if you did come back and couldn't find me?"

"I was so ashamed, Susanna." His voice broke, and to give himself a moment, he took a sip of lemonade, too. "I'd thrown away a real love for what? Some boy's dream?" Shaking his head at himself, he went on, "I can't tell you what went through my mind—my heart—when I saw you standing right here, that day we turned out the Eicher herd. It's a wonder I didn't ride right into the creek."

"You didn't even look at me," she accused. "Mind you, I wanted to run into the house so you wouldn't."

"Oh, I saw you, all right. And then when you drove the buggy into Josh and Sara's yard and the blizzard was already starting ... well, we both know what happened there. I got a revelation from *der Herr* that was like a thunderbolt. And I made up my mind to try again."

"He brought us together a second time," she said, slipping her hand into his, and leaning on his broad, dependable shoulder. "How can we ever be worthy of mercy like that?"

"Well, that's the thing about mercy," he said comfortably as their hands fit together like two halves made whole. "It's not because we're worthy. It's because God is worthy—of our thanks, our praise, of our very lives."

"I have a lot to thank Him for," she whispered.

"Me, too. As long as I can spend that life with you." He gripped her hand more tightly. "I don't want to waste any more time coming to an understanding. Unless that's what you want."

She shook her head. "I've waited long enough. Months and months too long. I don't want to be courted. I just want you."

He hitched his chair even closer and leaned his forehead on hers. "So you won't think I'm being too forward?"

"I could never accuse you of that. You're just obeying *Gott*'s timing."

"Then will you marry me?"

"*Ja*. Would tomorrow be all right?"

He tipped back his head and laughed, the way she hadn't heard him laugh in months and months. How she loved that sound!

Then, still chuckling, he wrapped her hand in his, and kissed each finger, one at a time. "The sooner the better, I say. But maybe after your Mamm and Luke's wedding in October. Can you wait that long?"

"As long as we're together, it won't be waiting. It'll be preparing for a life together."

And as he tipped up her chin with his free hand and his lips found hers, she thought her heart might burst with happiness. As far as she was concerned, a lifetime of thanking *Gott* for his mercy in bringing them together again had already begun.

EPILOGUE

BENNY SLID the last couple of feet out of their tunnel through the wild rosebushes and down to the narrow, grassy creek bank. They'd been working on the secret passage since they'd moved here, starting behind the chicken house and ending up on their very own private beach. Grass grew on a piece of the bank just the right height to make a seat, and a little bit of sand made swimming easy.

Gracie turned at his unexpected—and empty-handed—reappearance. "I thought you were getting some cookies."

"They're *kissing*. Aendi Susanna and *Stephen*." Benny made a face. "They're sitting at the table between us and the kitchen door, and they'd notice for sure and certain if I took some of their strawberries."

"I bet they wouldn't," Gracie said with infinite female wisdom. "Not if they were kissing."

"It's like before, at the Four Winds. Except I hope he won't go away again. Aendi Susanna was so crabby and weepy last time."

"I hope so, too." She loved her aunt, and it had upset her to hear the soft sounds of weeping in the middle of the night when she got up to get a drink out of the tap.

It wasn't as awful as the sound of Dat weeping, though. That was the absolute worst. Dat was the best father in the whole world, and if she could, Gracie would give him the moon and the stars in her cupped hands to make him feel better. He couldn't help it that Mamm had gone to heaven to be with *Gott*. He'd explained it to her once—how a person could be happy that the one they loved was in heaven, singing praises to *Gott* with all the *Engel*, but at the same time miss them so much it was like a big hole inside them.

Gracie was glad Stephen hadn't accidentally been taken up to heaven while he was away. Maybe the hole inside Aendi Susanna might be filled now. "Maybe they're going to get married."

"Ewww. Even more kissing."

"Better kissing than crying."

Benny shuddered and splashed his feet in the water. Then his sharp eyes caught something. "What's that?"

"It's a trout," she said dryly. "They live in here. Until a fisherman comes along and catches them."

"No, *that*." He waded in, soaking the turned-up cuffs of his pants, then soaked his shirt to the shoulder reaching down into the rushing water.

"If you slip on a rock and fall in, I'm not jumping in to rescue you," she informed him. The creek was cold, especially with all the snowmelt.

"I won't fall in. Look what I found!" He waded to the bank and plopped himself down beside her, soaking the whole side of her dress.

"Benny!"

"Look." He opened his hand. "Treasure."

"My goodness!" Her wet skirt forgotten, she took the plain gold ring and turned it around and around. It wasn't fancy with turquoise or coral like the ones in the window of the jewelry store in town, but something was written inside it. "I can't read it. It's in writing, and we won't learn that until school starts." She handed it back. "It's worldly, anyhow. Better throw it back." Like a trout too small to cook, it wasn't useful, and keeping it would be a sin.

"Someone's lost it. We could try to get it back to them."

"It could have been there for a hundred years. That's how long the Inn has been here. Dat said."

"I'm going to show him when he gets home."

"Why didn't he take us with him?" Gracie asked the creek crossly. It whispered, but had no answers. "He was supposed to go right past the Bar K, wasn't he? To bring that lady some more little trees."

"Maybe he'll stop and talk to Sylvia and she'll tell him he should have brought us. She always wants to see us."

Gracie hoped so. The mention of her name made her feel not so cross. "I like Sylvia. She never tells us we should be seen and not heard."

"I don't even know what that means," Benny complained. "Why do people say that?"

Gracie shook her head. "And she makes really *gut* ginger-bread cake." Her favorite.

"And peanut butter cookies." His favorite.

"And dumplings this big." Gracie made a fist. "I wish she was our *mamm*."

Benny looked a little shocked. "What about Mammi?"

"Mammi is … Mammi. And we love her forever and ever. But other kids have a father and a mother. Dat is lonely."

"How do you know? He has us. And Seth and Gid and Mammi and Susanna."

"But he's not like he was when Mamm was alive."

Even Benny had to admit this was true. "How is he going to find a *Fraa*, though? All he does is work and come home to do things with us."

Gracie was already thinking hard. "Church Sunday is going to be at Yoders' next door. And the barn raising is next week. Sylvia will be coming." When Benny gave her his *what are you up to now?* stare that looked just like Dat's, she said, "Well? If we don't do something, she might marry someone else."

"No one is better than Dat," Benny said loyally. "All right. What are we going to do?"

"Well, I haven't thought that up yet, have I?" She splashed her feet in the water. "But we have until Sunday to think up a plan." They were good at plans, though sometimes they came up with faulty ones and Mammi and Susanna got mad at them. "If we can get Dat to marry our favorite *Maedsche* in the whole valley, then—"

Benny was trying to toss the ring over a tiny stone up the bank, like playing horseshoes. But he still knew what she was going to say. "—then even Mammi will have to admit how *gut* we are."

Exactly. You just watch us, Gracie said in her mind to her family. This was going to be fun.

And Dat would be happy again.

THE END

AFTERWORD
A NOTE FROM ADINA

I hope you've enjoyed the eighth book about the Miller family of Mountain Home, Montana. If you subscribe to my newsletter, you'll hear about new releases in the series, my research in Montana, and snippets about quilting and writing and chickens—my favorite subjects!

I hope you'll join me by subscribing at:

https://www.subscribepage.com/shelley-adina

Haven't read the first book in the Amish Cowboys of Montana? Pick up *The Amish Cowboy* ebook for free on my store, www.moonshellbooks.com. And while you're there, be sure to browse my other Amish novels set in beautiful Whinburg Township, Pennsylvania, beginning with *The Wounded Heart*.

Turn the page for a glossary of the Pennsylvania Dutch words used in this book. But first, here's a sneak peek at Tobias's book, *The Amish Cowboy's Little Matchmakers*, book nine of The Amish Cowboys of Montana series!

The Amish Cowboy's Little Matchmakers
© Adina Senft

Expect double trouble when the Miller twins try to make a match for their father...

Widower Tobias Miller's seven-year-old twins are almost more than the exhausted wrangler can handle. Not only is he helping his mother and sister run the Wild Rose Amish Inn, but he also works part time at Mountain Home Feed and helps out on any ranch that needs another hand. So it's a gift from *Gott* when Sylvia Keim offers to look after the children until school starts. She has such a gentle spirit, and is so capable he could almost hug her ... if his love for his late wife wasn't still burning in his heart.

Sylvia Keim is older than many of the *Youngie* in Mountain Home, and her marriage prospects seem to diminish with every year, despite her mother's efforts to match her up with one of the Zook brothers—who are in their fifties. Tobias Miller's children are a handful, but she loves them anyway. Nor can she help her feelings for their father—grieving, over-whelmed, and yet so kind and so good with them that it's all she can do not to fall in love completely. Unrequited love would only lead to heartbreak, though, because Tobias never seems to see her past the shadow of his wife's memory.

What will it take for two lonely people to see how perfect they are for each other? Why, a little matchmaking from a pair of mischievous twins who want Sylvia to be their new *Mamm*, of course!

The Montana Millers. They believe in faith, family, and the land. They'll need all three when love comes to Mountain Home!

Find your copy of The Amish Cowboy's Little Matchmakers at your favorite online retailer, or in my store!

GLOSSARY

Spelling and definitions from Eugene S. Stine, *Pennsylvania German Dictionary* (Birdboro, PA: Pennsylvania German Society, 1996).

Words used:
Aendi: auntie
Ausbund: the Amish hymnal
Bidde: please
Boppli(n): baby, babies
Bruder: brother
Dat: Dad
Deitsch: Pennsylvania Dutch
Demut: humility
Denkes, mei Vater: My thanks, my Father
denki: thanks
Dochsder(e): daughter, daughters
druwwel-macher: troublemaker
Eck: corner, esp wedding table
eenzich: single

Engel: angels

Englisch: not-Amish people, English language

Erdgeischt: lit. "earth spirit," or gnome

der Herr: the Lord

Fraa: wife

Gmay: congregation, church body

Gott: God

Gott's wille: God's will

Grossmammi: great-grandmother

Guder owed: Good afternoon/evening

Guder mariye: Good morning

Guder nacht: Good night

gut: good

Hatge, mei friend: good-bye, my friend

Haus: house

hoch Deutsch: high German

hochmut: pride

im e familye weg: in the family way

Ischt okay: It's okay

ja: yes

Kaffee: coffee

Kapp: women's prayer covering

Kind, Kinner: child, children

kumm inne: come in

kumm mit: come along (lit. come with)

Ich liebe dich: I love you

Ich verstehe nicht: I don't understand

Liebe: love

Lieber Gott: dear God

Liewi: dear

Maedsche(r): girl, girls

Mamm: Mom

Mammi: Grandma

mei: my

mei Vater: My Father (God)

die Meinding: the *Bann*, or shunning

Narr: idiot

neh: no

Nix? From *nichts*, Is it not? Or No?

Rumspringe: the time for Amish teenagers to run around

Ordnung: discipline, or standard of behavior and dress unique to each community

Schtrimpe: socks

Schulhaus: schoolhouse

verhuddelt: confused, mixed up

wunderbaar: wonderful

Youngie: young people

ALSO BY ADINA SENFT

Amish Cowboys of Montana

The Amish Cowboy's Christmas prequel novella

The Amish Cowboy

The Amish Cowboy's Baby

The Amish Cowboy's Bride

The Amish Cowboy's Letter

The Amish Cowboy's Makeover

The Amish Cowboy's Home

The Amish Cowboy's Refuge

The Amish Cowboy's Mistake

The Amish Cowboy's Little Matchmakers

The Amish Cowboy's Wedding Quilt

The Amish Cowboy's Journey

❧

The Whinburg Township Amish

The Wounded Heart

The Hidden Life

The Tempted Soul

Herb of Grace

Keys of Heaven

Balm of Gilead

The Longest Road

The Highest Mountain

The Sweetest Song

The Heart's Return (novella)

❧

Smoke River

Grounds to Believe

Pocketful of Pearls

The Sound of Your Voice

Over Her Head

❧

Glory Prep (faith-based young adult)

Glory Prep

The Fruit of My Lipstick

Be Strong and Curvaceous

Who Made You a Princess?

Tidings of Great Boys

The Chic Shall Inherit the Earth

ABOUT THE AUTHOR

USA Today bestselling author Adina Senft grew up in a plain house church, where she was often asked by outsiders if she was Amish (the answer was no). She holds a PhD in Creative Writing from Lancaster University in the UK. Adina was the winner of RWA's RITA Award for Best Inspirational Novel in 2005, a finalist for that award in 2006, and was a Christy Award finalist in 2009. She appeared in the 2016 documentary film *Love Between the Covers*, is a popular speaker and convention panelist, and has been a guest on many podcasts, including Worldshapers and Realm of Books.

She writes steampunk adventure and mystery as Shelley Adina; and as Charlotte Henry, writes classic Regency romance. When she's not writing, Adina is usually quilting, sewing historical costumes, or enjoying the garden with her flock of rescued chickens.

Adina loves to talk with readers about books, quilting, and chickens!
www.moonshellbooks.com

facebook.com/adinasenft
x.com/shelleyadina
pinterest.com/shelleyadina
bookbub.com/authors/adina-senft
instagram.com/shelleyadinasenft

Made in the USA
Middletown, DE
10 September 2024

60627410R00146